KU-487-442

SECRET IN SILVER

SECRET IN SILVER

by
JOAN EATON

VICTORY PRESS
EASTBOURNE

ISBN 0 85476 214 0

Printed in Great Britain for
VICTORY PRESS (Evangelical Publishers Ltd.),
Lottbridge Drove, Eastbourne, Sussex,
by Richard Clay (The Chaucer Press) Ltd.,
Bungay, Suffolk.

CHAPTER ONE

THE QUARREL

"Jo! Jo! Where are you?"

The shrill voice came from across the field where the caravans were, but the tall girl, sitting alone on the gate, pretended not to hear. Her thick brown hair, hanging below her waist, completely hid her small discontented face. She was feeling in a bad mood and she wanted to be alone.

Vaguely she had been wondering why, as a little child, she had so much enjoyed the fun and thrills of a travelling fair. Now all the excitement she had felt had changed to boredom.

"Jo! Jo!" the voice repeated. "I see where you are, so you needn't make out you're dumb."

Jo pushed the hair away from her eyes, and noticed with annoyance that Gloria was coming towards her. Moreover, she was wearing a pink dress instead of her usual jersey and jeans.

Another party, I suppose, thought Jo. Secretly she was jealous of Gloria, with her round, rosy face, neat dark curls and sparkling black eyes. She could sing and dance and play the guitar, and everyone seemed to admire her.

As Gloria came nearer, Jo thought how light and graceful she was—almost like a fairy. She reached the middle of the field where the land sloped down to a muddy swamp, and picked her way daintily across on firm ground, without dirtying her feet. By the time she had reached the gate and had climbed on to it, Jo had pushed her hair over her face again, and was staring down at the grass beneath her.

The two girls sat in silence for some time. Gloria was the first to speak.

"You've been at it again. I saw you," she said.

Jo did not reply.

"Mum'll be mad with you," continued Gloria.

"She's gone to the market, so shut up!" snapped Jo at last. "I hoped you'd gone, too."

"Well, you'd better show me what you've done, anyway," said Gloria.

"No! I shan't!"

"If you don't, I'll tell Mum about you."

"I couldn't care less," Jo muttered.

"Oh come on," continued Gloria, coaxingly. "Let me see what it's all about. I'll give it back to you again. Really I will."

"Will you promise you won't spoil it, then?" asked Jo.

"Of course. Now do get a move on."

Slowly Jo drew out a sheet of paper from the pocket of her jeans, and, unfolding it, handed it to Gloria.

"My word!" exclaimed the latter, as she looked at the crayon sketch. "However do you do it, Jo? We don't need a photographer here. You've got us all into the picture, and the caravans and the animals, too. You'll have to give up drawing, though," she added. "It's no use to anyone—just a waste of time, really, and it only makes Mum angry with you."

"I couldn't care less," repeated Jo.

"Well, you should care," continued Gloria. "Mum was good to you, taking you in like she did when your own mum and dad were killed in that car crash."

"Of course she took me in," replied Jo. "My mum was her own sister, and she and my dad had helped her ever so much with the fair. She told me all that."

"And a fat lot you've done to help her in return," remarked Gloria. "If you hadn't been so clumsy and grown so big, you could have danced on the platform with me, and earned some cash. That's what Mum really wanted you to do, but there's too much of you. You're all arms and legs, aren't you, just like a daddy-long-legs?"

"Well, it's not my fault if I've grown more than you, and I'm glad I have," said Jo, crossly. "I'm stronger and I can run much faster, although I'm only just twelve and you're fourteen."

"Much good that'll do you when it comes to entertaining people," scoffed Gloria. "You aren't even musical enough to play the guitar. I'm going to be a pop singer when I grow up, and make lots of money."

"And I'm going to be an artist," remarked Jo.

"An artist!" exclaimed Gloria. "Of course you can't be one, you silly chump. Artists are no good at all. My friend, Poppy, knows all about them. They can't sell their pictures, she says, because no one wants them, and so they are always untidy and starving. They borrow other people's clothing to wear, and other people have to pay for their food."

"I don't believe they are all like that," replied Jo. "I shall meet some real artists one day and find out."

"But you can't make personal remarks and ask personal questions. People don't like it," said Gloria, in superior tones.

"What do you mean?" asked Jo.

"You baby! Don't you even know that? Well, if I told you that you had hair like tangled hay and a dirty face, and a hole in your jersey, that would be personal remarks. It would be true, too, but you wouldn't like it."

"Oh, stop it!" exclaimed Jo, feeling more and more angry. "I've had enough of you."

"You were supposed to clean the brass on the round-abouts this afternoon, and you haven't done a stroke of work," remarked Gloria. "You can do something for me, now. I'm going out to supper with Poppy tonight, and I want my shoes polished."

"I shan't polish your dirty shoes," exclaimed Jo, defiantly. "You can do them yourself."

"You saucy kid!" retorted Gloria, sliding down gracefully from the gate. "I'll make you sorry for being so rude."

Then, getting well out of Jo's reach, she tore up the sketch which she had been holding, and scattered the pieces on the ground.

"There," she added. "That serves you right."

For a moment Jo was speechless with surprise and dismay. Then her temper rose suddenly, and, in a voice which Gloria hardly recognised, she shouted, "You've broken your promise. You've spoilt my picture. I hate you. I'll pay you out for this."

Then, suddenly frightened, Gloria started running as fast as she could in the direction of the caravans. Meanwhile, Jo leapt down from the gate and went after her with long strides. It would not have taken her long to catch up with Gloria, but Jo had another idea. She kept just behind her till the girls reached the wettest part of the field. Then she gave her a sudden, violent push which sent her, face first, into a pool of muddy water.

Gloria picked herself up, spluttering and coughing, and then burst into angry tears.

"Oh, my dress, my pretty dress!" she wailed. "You horrible girl. I can't stand you. I'll tell Mum everything, and you'll catch it good and strong tonight."

Jo knew that punishment would follow; and two hours later, when she was sent to bed without tea or supper, and with the threat that next time she misbehaved she would get a sound beating, she was still angry and unrepentant.

"I'll never stop drawing pictures," she told herself, "and I'll never leave off hating Gloria, either."

CHAPTER TWO

ON THE FAIRGROUND

Bella Pickleworth walked slowly round the fairground in the warm, May twilight.

Her friends had often told her, in fun. that she was an older, stouter edition of her daughter. Certainly her hair and eyes were very like Gloria's, and in her younger days she, too, had been a graceful dancer with a pretty, musical voice.

She was feeling particularly annoyed that evening because her caravan, where she could usually enjoy some peace after the work of the day, was occupied by Gloria.

The two girls slept with her during the winter months, but as soon as the days became milder she rigged up a tent for them outside, so that she could have more room to spread herself, she told them. Whenever the girls had a quarrel, though, Gloria would leave the tent and go back to sleep with her mother, and Jo, on those occasions, was glad to be left alone.

Mrs. Pickleworth had had a tiring evening. Besides listening to all Gloria's complaints about Jo, she had made up a bed for her daughter in the caravan and washed all her muddy clothes.

"You'll have to send Jo to school tomorrow, Mum, and keep me at home with a bad cold and cough. Then we'll have some peace," Gloria had remarked.

'I daresay I'll send her off,' she had admitted, rather unwillingly.

Mrs. Pickleworth's opinion of 'schooling' had changed in recent years. When the girls were younger, she had been glad to be rid of them, and whenever she had moved to a new district her first thought had been to get them settled into a school. Regularly on Sunday afternoons, too, she had hurried them off to Sunday school so that she might have her afternoon nap.

Now it was rather different, though, for Gloria, at least, was becoming very useful to her on the fairground. Also, the fact that the girls were being taught to speak differently from the way she spoke annoyed her very much.

On one occasion. Gloria had actually corrected her, telling her that what she had said was not good grammar.

"Good grammar! Fiddlesticks!" she had retorted. "It's them schools, putting h'ideas into kids' 'eads an' making 'em too big for their boots. No h'airs an' graces with me, me girl! What's been good enough for me all along will be good enough for you, too."

Gloria hated lessons, and was actually backward for her age. She invented many clever excuses for being absent, and quite often Jo was sent off to school on her own. Jo, on the other hand, was quick to learn but always careful not to let Gloria know how much she enjoyed her lessons. The teachers in the different schools where she went were surprised that such an awkward, untidy girl could be so neat and painstaking in her work, and have so much talent for drawing.

I can't think why I be so daft as to keep this show going, Mrs. Pickleworth thought, as she returned from her stroll. I could sell up any day an' buy a bungalow and yet I don't do nothing about it.

This was true, for, although Mrs. Pickleworth had had a hard struggle to make a living after her husband had died, an elderly uncle had recently left her a large sum of money, and she was now comfortably off. She could not summon up enough courage yet, though, to give up the wandering life which she had known ever since she was a child.

She had, however, made some changes. The little circus which she had run in connection with the fair was now discontinued. The men in charge had been dismissed, and the ponies and the performing lions and bears had been sold. Only a small group of friends, who had helped her through difficult times, were now running the roundabouts and Dodgem cars for her, and looking after hoop-la and a few other games and stalls. As it was no longer essential for the fair to be profitable, Mrs. Pickleworth would close it and take a day off whenever she wished, and move on elsewhere when she felt so inclined.

Of course there was Mr. Farley, too. He was known affectionately as 'Granfer', and no one ever forgot that it was he who, through his wisdom and energy, had kept the show together during its most critical days. He was quite an old man now, and often ill, but Mrs. Pickleworth looked after him well. He had his own caravan as far away as possible from the noise and excitement of the fair, and nearly everyone, including Gloria and Jo, would visit him there, often asking his advice over different problems.

"Well, I'll get that lazy lass up to do the livestock tomorrow," Mrs. Pickleworth told herself as she passed Jo's tent and went back into her caravan. "Then I'll push her off to school."

Next morning, Jo was up early. For her it was a privilege and not a punishment to look after the animals and birds.

All the pets were small, easily managed ones, left over from the circus. There were three performing dogs called 'Salt', 'Pepper' and 'Mustard'. Salt was a little white terrier, Pepper a grey cairn and Mustard a Welsh corgi. They could dance on their hind legs, jump through hoops, take each other for rides in a toy cart and do many other clever things.

There were also two doves called 'Bill' and 'Coo',

and a pair of black and white rabbits. The doves and rabbits had often been used by Dick Rogers, the odd-job man, who was very clever at conjuring, and could make them come out of his pocket, or appear from under his hat when least expected.

The pet that Jo liked best of all, though, was Cocky, the handsome blue and yellow macaw. He had never forgotten that he had once belonged to a London news-agent, and when people came near him he would often shout out, "Evening piper! Evening piper!" in his Cockney accent.

Sometimes Mrs. Pickleworth would give a variety concert in a big marquee, and then all the pets would take part in it. On those occasions, Gloria would play her guitar and sing, while Mrs. Pickleworth and some of her friends joined in with the choruses.

The most important item on the programme, though, was Gloria's dance. She would come on to the platform in a crimson velvet dress and sparkling tiara, and with Cocky perched on her shoulder. He had been well trained, and was always quiet and on his best behaviour then. When the music started up for the dance, he would fly on to a perch behind her; and when the dance was over, he was back again on her shoulder. Then she would curtsey to the audience and come down from the platform while the people clapped and whistled and shouted for an encore.

Jo took the dogs for a good scamper through the fields that morning. Then she fed the rabbits and doves, and cleaned out the hutch and cage. She left Cocky to the last because she liked looking after him best. He lived in an enormous cage which was hung outside the pets' caravan.

"Evening piper! Evening piper!" he called out as she came up to him.

"Oh, Cocky, you're crazy!" she exclaimed, laughing.

"You haven't got a paper to sell me, and you know it isn't evening yet."

"Have a cup of tea, pretty dear," replied Cocky.

"I've had my cup of tea for breakfast already," said Jo, "and cornflakes and milk, too."

Cocky then remained silent for a while, watching her with his head on one side as she put some grit into his cage and filled up his bowl of water. Then suddenly he remarked, "Cheer up! Cocky's a lovely bird."

"I know you are, and here's your breakfast," said Jo, giving him nuts, seed and green food.

Cocky gave a high-pitched screech as he came down from his perch to inspect his meal.

"Cocky's got a sausage," he cried excitedly, and next moment he had picked up a brazil nut and cracked it with his powerful beak.

"Oh, Cocky!" exclaimed Jo, "I'd love to stay and watch you, but I've got to get ready for school. Say 'bye bye' then."

The macaw, however, was far too busy eating to pay any attention to Jo.

"Bye bye," she repeated. "Bye bye."

Cocky lifted up his head at last to give another raucous shriek, and then called out, "Happy Christmas, dear!"

"And the same to you, too," laughed Jo. "You silly bird!"

CHAPTER THREE

BLACK PRINCE

As Jo started off to school, she noticed Gloria's pink dress hanging out to dry. She felt sorry Aunt Bella had had the trouble of washing it. Why hadn't she made Gloria do it? she wondered.

Well, anyway, I'll have to do something kind for Aunt Bella to make up for this, she thought, and I'll pay Gloria out properly one day, too.

Just as school was finishing, Jo had an idea.

"Aunt Bella likes carrots," she said to herself, "and I know where there are lots."

She quickly put her books in her desk and left the school, carrying her empty satchel. On her way back she always passed a cottage, and she had heard that Miss Parsons, the old lady who lived there, was away for a week. She had noticed that in her neat little garden there was a row of early carrots.

Jo soon reached the cottage again and crept into the garden, making sure first that the old man she had sometimes seen working there had gone home. She then pulled up the whole row of carrots and found there was just enough room in her big satchel to take them all.

When she arrived at the fairground, she saw Mrs. Pickleworth standing outside her caravan.

'I'm back, Aunt Bella, and I've got a present for you," she announced.

"Carrots! Oh my! Ain't they fine ones, too," exclaimed Mrs. Pickleworth, and she did not ask Jo from where they had come. "Thank you, ducks. My stew'll taste fine tonight, I'll be bound," she added.

While Mrs. Pickleworth was in such a good mood,

Jo came out with a question that she had always wanted to ask.

"Aunt Bella," she said, "please can you tell me what my dad did to help you so much with the fair?"

Mrs. Pickleworth frowned. She never seemed to like answering questions.

"Well," she replied, "he was a trapeze artist, an' wonderful on the tight-rope, but that was a long while ago, when we was startin' the circus."

"And please, Aunt Bella, did my mum ever do any drawing or painting, just in her free time, I mean?"

"She did paintin', but no more than the sort that mattered," answered Mrs. Pickleworth.

"What sort was that?" asked Jo.

"Why, paintin' an' varnishin' gates and posts an' such like, of course," was the reply. "Now, that's enough natter! You go and take off yer school clothes an' get yerself some tea."

Jo went into the tent and found that Gloria had come back again, with all her belongings scattered around. She had forgotten all about the quarrel, and seemed very excited.

"Jo!" she exclaimed. "What do you think? Poppy's mum has asked me to sing at a concert quite soon! It will be in their village, and Poppy's dad will fetch me in his car."

"Oh," said Jo, not feeling at all interested.

"My name will be on all the programmes—'Gloria Ermintrude Pickleworth'—beautiful, isn't it, and sort of musical, too?"

"I'm not a bit struck," commented Jo.

"Well, you can't boast about your name, can you?" snapped Gloria. "Fancy your mum calling you just 'Jo' and nothing else!"

"But Jo is short for Josephine, I think," the other girl replied.

My mum said you were just Jo Plain," retorted

Gloria. "You don't need to make yourself look as plain as you do, though. I wouldn't mind having your blue eyes and black lashes, myself, but why can't you comb your hair and wash your face, and——"

"Oh, stop it!" interrupted Jo. Picking up a pillow, she was about to fling it at Gloria when the two girls heard an unfamiliar voice near their tent, and hurried out to see who the visitor might be.

Mrs. Pickleworth was standing beside a stout, short man who had just led in a handsome black pony.

"Coo! It's Farmer Burke, and one of our own circus ponies that Mum sold come back again, I do believe," said Gloria.

"And I'm sure it's the Black Prince!" cried Jo. "How simply super!"

Suddenly, the pony broke away, and, neighing loudly, trotted across the fairground.

"What's got 'old of 'im?" asked Mrs. Pickleworth.

"He's seen his old friend," replied the farmer, looking amused. "If I'm not much mistook, it's Tom Trent himself, that trained him for your circus."

"Ah, Tom; 'e's got a wonderful way with 'orses," said Mrs. Pickleworth, "—takes a dim view of them machines 'e works nowadays; but times must change, and us with it," she added, philosophically.

Meanwhile, Tom, a slim, dark-haired young man, came forward, followed by the excited pony.

"Oh, it's good to see the Black Prince again," he exclaimed; "and you're Farmer Burke that bought him, I should say. Are you wanting to sell him back to us?"

"Not on your life," replied the farmer. "The wife and kid's would never forgive me. It's just that we have found out that you've moved near us, and we want you to help us out of a jam. We've sold our farm—the offer came all of a sudden—and now we are off to Wales, looking at some cottages in the country. We'll be away at least five weeks, getting fixed up. The trouble is, we can't take Prince with us yet, and there's no one we can trust him with. Will you take him back, ma'am?" he added, turning to Mrs. Pickleworth. "He'd be in clover with you."

Mrs. Pickleworth looked very serious. "No clover round here," she said at last, taking the farmer's remark literally, "an' no permission for grazing 'orses, neither. If I took 'im, 'e'd 'ave to pay 'is way like the rest of us. Maybe 'e could earn 'is keep taking kids for rides after school, with Tom in charge of 'im."

"That's a fine idea," replied the farmer. "The exercise would be good for him, and he's wonderful with children; but I'll pay for his grain and everything else you say as well. I've brought you a truckful of hay, too, if you'll accept it."

"A truckful!" exclaimed Mrs. Pickleworth, "but 'e won't use all that in five weeks."

"Well, it's no good to us, as we're leaving, so if you'd like it——"

"I daresay I'd find a use for it. We don't waste nothin' 'ere," said Mrs. Pickleworth. "We can store it in an empty caravan."

At that moment, Salt, Pepper and Mustard came leaping forward with yelps of delight. Prince recognised them, and as he bent down to greet them they licked his head and his neck.

"Upon my word, he's glad to be back with all his pals around him!" exclaimed Farmer Burke.

"He's a wonderful pony," said Tom, who enjoyed talking about horses more than anything else. "He's the best I ever trained—so steady and sensible. There's one thing you should know, though. He's terrified of fireworks. Some lads let off a chinese cracker near him once, and he was just about crazy with fear. It upset him for days."

"What a daft thing to do!" cried the farmer, indignantly. "You'd think youngsters would have more sense. I can assure you we keep all our pets out of the way on bonfire night!"

"I suppose yer know, mister, we ain't got no stable for yer pony," Mrs. Pickleworth broke in.

"He won't need that. He's always outdoors in the summer. I'm sure he'll stay with you, but it might be best to tether him at night."

"We'll do that all right, an' we won't let 'im out of our sight in the daytime, neither," replied Mrs. Pickleworth.

"Well, I'm much obliged to you, I'm sure. My family would break their hearts if anything happened to him, and he couldn't be in a safer place than here."

"It will be grand looking after him, too, sir," said Tom enthusiastically. "I'd give a lot to go back to the old days. It's iron roundabout nags I take care of now, more's the pity."

"You girl's 'ad best 'elp unload that truck now," suggested Mrs. Pickleworth.

"I'll fetch young Jimmy, and the wife, too, and we can all lend a hand," said Tom.

Soon the hay was stored in a large yellow caravan, and later that afternoon Tom found a suitable place on the fairground where Prince could be tethered on a long rope. Jo came round then, with Bessie Trent and Jimmy, and gave the pony a lump of sugar.

Eight-year-old Jimmy, a wiry little boy with a mop of tight, black curls, was the youngest member of the party, and was very useful to his father in many ways, after school hours.

"Isn't Prince smashing, with his long mane and swishing tail," he exclaimed excitedly.

"I'll never forget how handsome he looked in the circus ring, with his golden bridle, and rosettes on his ears," replied Bessie.

Jo suddenly remembered that Granfer had perhaps

not heard of Prince's arrival, so she hurried over to his caravan to tell him everything.

The frail old man listened attentively to her news.

"Prince is really gorgeous," she exclaimed at last.

"And I suppose Cocky, the favourite, must now take a back seat," suggested Granfer, smiling.

"Oh no," replied Jo. "He's even gorgeouser." Then her face clouded over as she glanced out of the caravan window. "Gloria's coming to you," she announced grimly. "I'll have to bolt."

"But why?" asked Granfer.

"Because we are sick and tired of each other," was Jo's reply. "Anyway," she added with a grin, "I'm glad I got here first. Won't Gloria be mad when she finds what she wants to tell you is stale news!"

Prince settled down happily on the fairground, and became the centre of attraction. Jimmy told his school friends about him, and soon a number of young children were asking for riding lessons, which Tom fitted in for them before he became busy with the evening fair. Gloria, Jo and Jimmy were also allowed to ride the pony sometimes.

Jo had become less discontented, for she had at last discovered a way of continuing her sketching in secret. At least once every week she would ask Aunt Bella after school if she could go to the nearby woods and gather up firewood.

Mrs. Pickleworth was always delighted to lend her a big basket on these occasions, but she little knew that when the girl set out she had with her, carefully hidden under some newspapers, and old drawing book given her by a school friend, and a pencil, rubber and box of crayons.

Jo was always careful to fill her basket with sticks first. Then she would sit down on an old tree stump and start sketching the most exciting pictures. Sometimes she would draw the trees and flowers around her, and on other occasions strange imaginary scenes in cities and villages, and even fairy palaces.

"This is super," she told herself one day. "If Aunt Bella always wants sticks, I may have time to become a real artist."

CHAPTER FOUR

FIRE AT CAMP

One night, Gloria and Jo, sleeping peacefully in their tent, were awakened suddenly by loud, excited barking.

"Oh crumbs! I wish those dogs would shut up," muttered Gloria, sleepily. "I expect they are chasing a cat."

"Had I better go and see what's the matter?" asked Jo.

"No, Mum wouldn't like it," replied Gloria. "Someone is sure to get up soon and stop them. It's after midnight," she added, looking at her luminous watch, "and it's too bad of them, disturbing us like that."

The dogs became suddenly silent, and, listening very carefully, Jo thought she could just hear a faint murmur of voices.

The two girls turned over in bed and were soon fast asleep again. An hour later, however, they were awakened once more by loud and furious barking, and they sprang out of bed.

"There's something really wrong this time," said Jo.

"Yes," agreed Gloria. "I've never heard them make that noise before. We'd better put on our anoraks and wake up Tom or Dick or someone."

This, however, was unnecessary, for when the girls rushed out of their tent the whole party was up and about and noticing, in horror, the darting tongues of flame which were coming from a corner of the fairground. The yellow caravan which contained the hay was on fire, and blazing furiously.

There were cries of "Help! Fire! What can we do? We need the fire-engine. Quick, someone!" Then a calm voice seemed to rise above all the others, and there was Granfer, with an old rug draped over his shoulders, taking command of the whole situation.

"Act quickly and don't panic," he said. "We can't save the caravan, but we must stop the fire from spreading. Will the men move away everything near it. Bessie, take the Ford and drive to the nearest telephone box. Dial 999 and ask for the fire-engine. Will all the other ladies and Gloria, Jo and Jimmy get every bucket you can find, and spread out in a chain to the river. Start passing up water. The men will be ready to help you soon."

The whole party worked hard, keeping the fire under control till the firemen arrived and took over. "You've done a good job," one of them remarked. "Your caravan's a write-off, but there won't be any further damage."

A policeman then appeared on the scene. "Are you all safe?" he asked.

"Yes," replied Mrs. Pickleworth. "We're all 'ere."

"And the livestock?"

"They're okay, too. They're right at the far end," said Dick.

"And can anyone tell me how the fire started?"

Heads were shaken, and everyone murmured, "No."

"We put nothing inflammable in that caravan, officer," said Tom. "There was only very dry hay, and we packed it in ourselves."

The policeman then beckoned Mrs. Pickleworth aside. "Is there anyone in your party who might have set fire to it on purpose—maybe just for a lark?" he asked, quietly.

"Oh no, officer, there b'ain't no one would do a thing like that."

"And have you any enemies outside the camp who might want to do you harm?"

"Not that I know of," replied Mrs. Pickleworth,

feeling very worried and perplexed. "I just can't make out why——"

She did not finish the sentence, for Tom rushed up to her. "The Prince!" he groaned. "He's slipped his halter and gone!"

"No! No!" cried Mrs. Pickleworth, in real distress. "'e'll 'ave gone crazy with fright again, an' we'll never see 'im no more. Oh, officer," she implored, "you'll get 'im back for us, won't yer? 'E's worth thousands an' 'e ain't ours."

"We'll do our best," said the policeman, soothingly, "but I expect he'll turn up on his own, later."

"'E won't. 'E never will," cried Mrs. Pickleworth, despairingly.

"Well, there's no more we can do now at night," replied the policeman, "but I'll be back in the morning with some other chaps, and we'll try to sort things out then."

"We'd better all get some sleep now, if we can," said Bessie, wearily. "Come along, Jimmy."

As the girls walked back to their tent they met Granfer.

"You were just wonderful the way you got things going," Gloria exclaimed.

"If there had been a wind to spread the fire, and if we had had no good dogs to warn us, some of us might have been burned to death," replied the old man, solemnly. "I think we should all thank our heavenly father for looking after us so well, don't you?"

Jo felt uncomfortable. When she had been younger, she had thought a good deal about God and about Jesus Christ, God's Son, but lately she had seldom remembered even to say her prayers.

"Oh, Granfer, you are so much better at that kind of thing than we are," Gloria answered, carelessly. "I think you should say one big prayer for us all," she added, as she hurried off to bed.

The days which followed were unhappy ones for everybody at the camp. The mess which the fire had caused was soon cleared up, and even the cost of the burnt-out caravan was covered by insurance. What mattered far more, though, was the fact that Black Prince was still missing. The police made endless enquiries, and Tom hired a horse and rode far and wide in search of the pony, but all to no purpose.

Everyone looked tired and worried, and Mrs. Pickleworth decided to cancel the running of the evening fair for the time being. Even Jimmy had a pale face, and eyes which had become red with crying.

"I've never known the little lad so tender-hearted before," Bessie remarked one day to Ada, Dick Rogers' wife, "but then, he do love dumb creatures."

"And so do we all," replied Ada. "The trouble is, we know just nothing. Prince may even have been stolen by now."

"I still think he may be out on the moors," broke in Tom. "There are dozens of almost wild ponies there. Some are so like him that folk who don't know him as we do couldn't tell the difference. There's no need to worry on his account," he continued. "He'll find enough to eat and plenty of his own kind for company, too."

"It would be fine to be free all the time," sighed Jo, who was standing near. "Would he be happier if he was never caught again?"

"No, Jo," replied Tom. "Prince would have a tough time on the moors in the winter. When a lot of snow falls, even the wild ponies are in danger of starving. Food has to be dropped to them sometimes, by helicopter. I wish Farmer Burke had given us an address where we could write to him," he added. "He may be back in about ten days, and he's still no idea what's been happening."

There was another reason for anxiety at the camp,

for no one there had been able to find out how the fire had started. Mrs. Pickleworth became nervous, and insisted that every night one of her party should sit up and keep watch. "There's no tellin' the chap won't come back an' try more tricks on us," she remarked, grimly.

The feeling of tension had made the two girls even more quarrelsome than usual.

One evening, Gloria left her work-basket on the floor of the tent, and Jo kicked it over by mistake.

"Look what you've done, you clumsy clown!" exclaimed Gloria, crossly. "Why can't you keep your big feet out of the way?"

"I didn't do it on purpose," said Jo, "and you shouldn't have left it there, anyway."

Gloria was in a teasing mood, and after a short while remarked, "I've been wondering, Jo, what *you* were doing on the night of the fire. We both woke up at midnight, and I went to sleep again. I believe that you got up and set fire to the caravan at one o'clock. It's just the idiotic sort of trick you'd play on us."

Jo became crimson with fury. "I'd never do a thing like that," she cried, "and harm poor Prince, who's a thousand times nicer than you. I wish you'd gone away instead and got lost for ever. I wouldn't be surprised if you'd started the fire yourself, in your mean, sneaky way."

"How dare you speak to me like that, you cheeky brat!" retorted Gloria, and she dodged out of the way quickly as Jo picked up her hair-brush and hurled it at her.

Gloria was terrified of Jo when she was in a temper. "Stop it! Stop it!" she shouted. "If you do anything to me, I'll yell out to Mum."

"An' if you two kids don't stop scrappin', I'll knock yer 'eads together," came Mrs. Pickleworth's angry voice from outside. "I won't stand no more."

Gloria and Jo scowled at each other and undressed in silence.

The following afternoon, when they had just returned from school, Bessie came rushing up to Mrs. Pickleworth. "Tom's ridden to the old farm where the Burkes lived, to see if the pony has gone back there," she explained, "but the postman, who knows our Prince, says he's pretty sure he saw him just now. He's a mile from here, on the edge of the moor with two other ponies. I'd go after him like a shot, but he knows the girls best as they ride him. Do you think they could try and bring him back?"

"But this is just wonderful!" exclaimed Mrs. Pickleworth. "They shall go at once."

"I've brought along his halter and some sugar and oats they can take to entice him," continued Bessie, "and it was just near the old, broken gate where he was seen."

Jo felt a thrill of excitement. Then, suddenly, Gloria said, "If Jo comes, can you stop her trampling about like a herd of wild elephants, Mum? I'm afraid she'll scare Prince away."

Mrs. Pickleworth looked worried. "We must get that pony back," she replied. "Maybe it would be best for just one of you to go. Jo can come an' 'elp me instead."

As Jo followed Aunt Bella into her caravan, hot angry tears sprang up in her eyes, but she blinked them back again. She was not going to let anyone know how bitterly disappointed she was, but some day she hoped to pay Gloria out. She could wait, though, till she could think of something really bad enough to do to her.

There was great disappointment in the camp an hour later when Gloria returned without the pony. "It was Prince all right," she said, "but his eyes were wild with fear and he didn't seem to know me. I showed him what I'd brought, but he wouldn't come near me, and then something scared him, and he galloped right away, out of sight, with the other ponies."

"Can I go and look for him now?" asked Jo.

"Yes, if you want to," replied Aunt Bella, sadly, "though I don't reckon it'll make much odds."

Jo ran nearly all the way, and soon reached the place where the pony had been seen. It was all very beautiful there, with gorse bushes shining like gold in the evening light, and the open moor stretching on and on into the distance. There was no Prince, nor any other pony in sight, though, and reluctantly the girl returned to the camp.

Next day, and for a whole week afterwards, Tom rode across the moor in search of Prince, but without success. "It's five weeks now since the farmer left, and he could turn up any time," he remarked, miserably, one evening.

Mrs. Pickleworth, also, was becoming more and more depressed, and so she was not in the best of moods one morning when Jimmy and three other small boys called at her caravan.

"What's all this in aid of?" she asked, rather crossly. "If you think I'm playing Fairy Godmother, 'andin' round balloons an' h'oranges, yer mistook."

"It's not that," said Jimmy, in a very frightened voice. "You see, we've all come to say something."

"Why don't yer say it, then?" asked Mrs Pickleworth impatiently. Then, seeing Tom near, she called out, "Do come along an' see what young Jimmy an' 'is pals want."

Tom came forward. "Well, son," he said, "what's all this about?"

"Granfer told us to come, Dad," Jimmy began. "We're very sorry, but we had a midnight feast, and——"

"A midnight feast?" repeated Tom. "We never

heard you get up, or these other chaps arrive. When did you have it? Was it last night?"

"No," continued another boy. "We wanted to be grown up, so I brought along some of my dad's cigarettes. We started smoking, but we didn't like it at all."

"But when did you do all this?" asked Tom again.

"On that night, in the yellow caravan," replied Jimmy, trembling all over. "We got scared all at once, and ran back. We hid the cigarettes in the hay, and we thought they had all gone out."

"So it was you that started the fire!" exclaimed Mrs. Pickleworth, very deeply shocked and yet, at the same time, relieved that the mystery had at last been cleared up.

"And why didn't you own up at once?" asked Tom, in very angry tones.

"I was too scared. I didn't tell anyone," said Jimmy, "but Granfer guessed, and told us all to come."

"Well," reflected Tom, sternly, "I am thoroughly ashamed of you, Jimmy. There will be no more pocket-money for you till that pony's found, and I hope your school mates will have none from their dads, either. You deserve a worse punishment than that, though, and I shall make sure that you get it."

"No, Tom," said Granfer, coming forward suddenly. "One punishment is enough. This lad, and most likely the others, too, has been punished ever since the fire began. I could see all the trouble in Jimmy's face. They meant no real harm. Let them just go without their money, That's enough."

"But we don't want any money, anyway," sobbed Jimmy. "We only want Prince to come back."

CHAPTER FIVE

AT THE SUPERMARKET

Two days after Jimmy's confession, Gloria announced to Jo, when school was over, that she and Poppy were going to a party together.

"I'll make myself look pretty, first," she said, "and then we'll meet in the town. I suppose you'll be picking up sticks for Mum?" she added, pityingly.

"I suppose I shall," answered Jo, brightly. She had remembered with pleasure that the last time she had gone to the woods she had caught a fleeting glimpse of a magnificent stag. It had bounded across the path, and since then she had been hoping to see it again, and perhaps even have time to draw it.

An hour later, her basket already full of sticks, she crept to the more open part of the wood, where she had seen the deer, and took up her position under a tall beech tree. She sat there motionless, her paper and pencil near her.

I'm being rather silly, she thought, after a while. I ought to know by now that wild animals don't come just when you want them. If only a squirrel or a rabbit would show itself, though, it would be something.

She took an apple out of her pocket and started to munch it. Then, suddenly, she heard a rustling in the undergrowth behind her, and a heavy tread.

It must be a big animal to make all that noise, she thought. It really is the stag, then, and he's coming this way! I must keep ever so still.

This was not easy, for she was trembling all over with excitement.

The steps sounded very near now, but, just when she thought the animal would pass in front of her, it stopped. Jo could bear the suspense no longer. She turned round very cautiously, and there, standing just behind her, she saw, to her astonishment, no graceful stag, but a black pony with a shaggy mane and a long tail.

"Prince," she exclaimed in delight. "Is it really you?"

She stretched out her hand, but the pony tossed his head and backed into a thicket.

"All right, my beauty," said Jo. "I won't try and hurry you. You had a bad fright, didn't you? Well, I was scared stiff, too, but I didn't run away. Now it's all over, and we'll soon go back together."

She continued talking to him for some time, and, growing used to the sound of her voice, he began walking towards her again.

"I suppose you want my apple," she said, putting it down on her lap, "but you'll have to fetch it yourself, if you do."

The pony came closer, gaining confidence with every step. Then, as he bent his long neck and helped himself to the fruit, he allowed Jo to stroke him. All fear had left him. He had forgotten the past nightmare, and was living again in what seemed a familiar and happy present.

Jo took a very thin, worn piece of string from her pocket and put it round the pony's neck. "I haven't a halter for you," she said, "and you needn't be scared of this. You could break it in a minute and get away again if you wanted to."

To her delight, however, the pony allowed himself to be led through the wood and out on to the road. He followed her quietly till he saw, on the left-hand side, a little white gate leading into a field. Here he stopped suddenly and refused to go any further.

"Prince, what's the matter?" cried Jo in dismay. "You've been here before, and this is the gate where I used to tie you while I picked flowers in the field. Can't you remember? And it was here that I used to ride you again." Then, as a happy thought struck her, she exclaimed, "Oh, Prince! Are you really waiting for me to ride you now?"

The next moment she had mounted the pony, and to her great joy he started trotting happily towards the fairground.

I've forgotten all about my basket of sticks, thought Jo, but who cares? I can fetch it later.

As they turned a corner, they came suddenly face to face with Gloria, who was on her way to the town. She looked at them in astonishment. Then her face clouded over.

"I've got Prince!" Jo shouted triumphantly.

"So I see," Gloria replied, without enthusiasm. "It's a good job he's turned up, but I expect he was on his way back, anyway. Animals always come home when they are hungry, you know—cats and dogs and everything."

A tremendous welcome awaited Jo and Prince at the fairground. Everyone crowded round with exclamations of surprise and delight. Jimmy flung his arms round the pony's neck Tom patted Jo on the back, and Mrs. Pickleworth exclaimed, "You've done a real good turn today, ducks, an' I'm proud of you."

Then, by some strange coincidence, a few minutes later Farmer Burke arrived. Prince recognised his master at once. Neighing excitedly, and with Jo still on his back, he cantered across the fairground to welcome him.

"Prince, my old pal, and aren't I glad to see you again!" exclaimed the delighted farmer, as he caressed the pony. "Looks as though you've been exercised all day long, my beauty." Then, turning to Mrs. Pickleworth, he continued, "I am more grateful to you all than I can tell you, ma'am. Sorry I have to take him away in such a rush, but I've been promised the loan of a horse-box if I can get to the village quickly. Got a splendid home in Wales. He'll be happy as a king there, and——"

"But Mr. Burke," cried Mrs. Pickleworth, "I want yer to know what's bin' 'appening to 'im all these days."

"I'd like to hear all about him. Indeed I would. But I daren't stop a minute now. Tom, please fetch his bridle."

"But, sir!" exclaimed Tom, "we must tell you first——"

"I know," interrupted the farmer, "you are thinking about his food and drink, aren't you? He'll get it all, I promise you, and a bit of a brush-up later, too. I don't want to miss that horse-box, though, so I do beg you to hurry."

While the bewildered Tom was putting on Prince's bridle, Farmer Burke handed an envelope to Mrs. Pickleworth. "Here's my cheque," he said, "and I'm so much obliged to you. Next time we go away, we'll bring Prince to you again."

"But, mister,' cried Mrs. Pickleworth in despair. "You don't give me time to explain. I'll have to get Tom to write to yer."

"A fine idea; we'd like to hear from him. And as for you, young lady," the farmer continued, turning to Jo, "you've got wonderful control of that pony. My kids will be green with envy when they hear that you ride him without saddle or bridle. Now, goodbye to you all," he added, "and a thousand thanks."

Next moment, Farmer Burke, leading Prince, had crossed the fairground and was out of sight.

Overcome with mingled feelings of surprise, relief and bewilderment, Mrs. Pickleworth sat down heavily on the ground. "Well, if that don't beat everything!" she gasped.

Although Jo was sorry Prince had been taken away, she felt satisfied and rather important, too, during the next few days. People kept congratulating her on having brought back the pony, and she enjoyed the praise which so seldom came her way.

A big disappointment awaited her one evening soon afterwards, however. She had planned to go to the woods again, but, when she asked for the basket for the sticks, Aunt Bella replied, "We don't need no more wood; we're chock-a-block. But you can 'elp me with the polishin'. Fair starts up again tomorrow."

Jo hated cleaning and polishing, and when she went off to bed that night she was feeling really angry. She found Gloria sitting on her camp bed with a mirror in her hand, and as she stepped past her she gave her a slap on the back.

"Oh, do stop it!" said Gloria, more agreeably than usual. "Don't let's start another scrap. I've got something to show you. I was just going to try it on when you came in."

She drew out of her pocket a necklace of red, gold and silver beads.

"Aren't they super!" she exclaimed, "and just what I need to wear with my red dress for the concert."

A sudden thought of revenge came to Jo. The red dress! Yes, the red dress which meant so much to Gloria. She would cut holes in it to pay her out for tearing up her picture, and for so often spoiling her fun.

Aunt Bella looked after this special dress in her caravan, though, so she would have to wait till it was brought out, just before the concert.

"Well, aren't you going to ask me where I got this gorgeous necklace?" said Gloria.

"I don't know," replied Jo, absently.

"Have a guess, then."

"I suppose Poppy gave it to you."

"No, she didn't. It's too nice. She would have kept it for herself. Well, I helped myself to it, if you want to know."

"Helped yourself to it? What do you mean?" asked Jo, feeling interested at last.

"I just took it, or, to use grander words, I shop-lifted it from the supermarket."

"Crumbs! How did you dare?" exclaimed Jo.

"Oh, it's easy enough for me," said Gloria. "I helped myself to a basket and went round to choose a postcard, and when no one was looking I slipped the necklace into my pocket. Then, when I paid for the postcard, I gave the lady a sweet smile and said, 'Thank you', and she just thought, What a pretty girl and what nice manners. It wouldn't do for you to try, though," continued Gloria. "You're so clumsy, you'd be sure to get caught and bring disgrace on us all. Mum would be angry even if she knew I'd done it. You've got to promise not to tell her."

"All right, I promise," said Jo, dreamily, for her thoughts had now wandered away to the supermarket where, on a stationery shelf, she had noticed some beautiful paint boxes. Jo longed for a nice one of her own, but Aunt Bella had refused to spend money on something which she considered so useless. The girl had had to make do with an old one which a teacher had found her, and from which, unfortunately, several colours were missing.

I'll get a new one after school tomorrow, Jo thought. If Gloria can manage that sort of thing, I can do it, too.

It was very near closing time when Jo arrived at the supermarket the next day. She decided she would go in at the main entrance and walk through the shop, looking at different articles. Then, when she was sure no one was noticing her, she would snatch the paint-box, slip it under her coat, and go out the back way. She needed an excuse, though, for going into the shop, and as, unlike Gloria, she had no money to spend, she would have to ask for something which she could be sure would not be in stock.

There were very few people in the store that evening. A few late customers were doing some hurried shopping, and an old man was standing near one of the entrances, reading a newspaper. Most of the assistants seemed to be tidying up the place, and one of them was sweeping the floor.

"Are there any ripe figs, please?" Jo asked one of the women near the fruit stall.

"Sorry love, it's too soon, and anyway, we don't often get them," was the reply.

Jo walked slowly then towards the stationery department. Her face was flushed and her legs were shaking under her. She must wait, she knew, for the right opportunity.

Suddenly a young woman hurried into the shop, carying an enormously fat baby with a very pink face and yellow curls. Immediately, all eyes seemed to turn in that direction, and there were exclamations of "Oh, you little dear!" "Aren't you lovely!" "Mummy's booful boy!"

Surely this was the right moment, and so, just as a voice was saying, "And now, my precious, you show all these kind aunties your two new toofy-pegs", Jo picked up a paint-box and hid it quickly under her coat. Then she walked as steadily as she could through the back entrance of the shop.

The lane along which she then crept was not used very much, and there seemed to be no one about. She knew, however, that it would not be wise to hurry, as this might arouse suspicion.

Suddenly she heard quick footsteps behind her, and a strong hand took hold of her arm. Trembling all over, she turned round and recognised the old man whom she had noticed reading a newspaper.

"You must come back to the store, young lady," he said in rather a stern voice. "I saw you take it. Now hand it over to me, please."

Feeling quite terrified, she drew out the paint-box and gave it to him.

"You know this is stealing," he continued. "What are your father and mother going to say when they know you have been handed over to the police?"

"They are both dead," Jo blurted out.

"Who looks after you, then, and where do you come from?" he asked in rather more gentle tones.

"My aunt does, and we live on the fairground," answered Jo.

"And I wonder what your aunt will say when she knows about this?"

Jo suddenly burst into tears.

"You are crying, aren't you, because you think you will have a good beating?" suggested the old man.

Jo wiped her eyes. "No," she answered, "I'll get a beating all right, but I'm not crying because of that. It's because my aunt will never let me paint again."

"You like painting very much, then?"

"Oh yes," agreed Jo. "I like it better than anything else."

The old man was puzzled. Until recently he had been the minister of a local church, and had helped many young people. But this girl seemed so different from the other children he had dealt with. Moreover, he did not approve of girls being beaten. "I wonder," he said to himself, "if I can possibly help her and put her on the right path."

Jo was surprised at the long silence.

"What's your name?" he asked at last.

"Jo Plain," she answered.

"And I am Mr White," he said. "Now listen, Jo, I am not the supermarket detective who visits the shop on certain days. If I were, it would be my duty to in-form the police about you. I happened, however, to be just an ordinary customer there, this evening, and it was only by chance that I saw what you did. I may be acting foolishly, but I feel inclined to take the paint-box back myself, and, as the manager and I are friends, I think he will agree with me that you need not be reported this time."

"Oh, Mr. White," exclaimed Jo, in relief, "do you mean you are going to let me off?"

"Under certain conditions," said Mr. White. "I shall need two promises from you. First of all, do you know the little hall next to the church in Light Street?"

"Yes, I know where you mean."

"I take a class of girls and boys there every Sunday afternoon at three o'clock," continued Mr. White. "I want you to come to it next Sunday and to arrive at half past two, so that I can talk to you privately first. Will you do that?"

"Oh yes," said Jo, eagerly. "I will, really."

"And then," continued Mr. White, "I want you also to promise most solemnly that you will never again take anything that does not belong to you."

Mr. White noticed a troubled expression on Jo's face.

"I'll never steal anything from shops again," she said, "but I can't promise I won't take little things like fruit out of people's gardens. My friends all do that, and I couldn't be different from them."

"Our Lord requires us to be honest and true over the little things as well as the big ones," said Mr. White. "However, that is a problem we must sort out together next Sunday. Now I am relying on you to keep your word. You won't let me down, will you?"

"Oh no," replied Jo. "I promise you I'll come."

CHAPTER SIX

JO'S DECISION

At five and twenty minutes past two on the following Sunday afternoon, Mr. White was waiting anxiously in the little hall. Had he really been wise in trusting that girl to keep her appointment? he wondered. At exactly half past two, however, Jo arrived, in her best clothes and with her hair tied back in a neat pony tail.

"I am so glad you have come," he said. "Now sit down and make yourself comfortable. I want to ask you first if you have ever been to a Bible class or Sunday school before."

"Oh yes," said Jo. "I've been for years. It is only since last summer that I left off."

"Then you know that Jesus Christ came down into the world and set us a perfect example of the way we should live?"

"Yes, the teacher told us lots of stories about Him."

"Surely, you know, then, that it is not right to tell lies and steal?"

"But I never tell lies," replied Jo. "People wouldn't believe me next time, if I did, and I wouldn't like that."

"What about stealing, then?" asked Mr. White. "One of God's Ten Commandments tells us not to do so, and Jesus, in His teaching, has shown us how wrong it is. Why do you steal?"

"I've never stolen anything big except that paint-box. It's only little things," said Jo.

"But stealing little things is as dishonest as stealing big ones. Our Lord's standard is high for those who belong to Him."

"I know," agreed Jo. "That's why I left off going to Sunday school."

"What do you mean?" asked the old man.

"It is hard to explain," Jo answered, "but the Sunday school teacher at the place where we were last summer told us that, because Jesus died for us all, we could be forgiven and belong to Him if we did what He asked us to do. I wanted to belong to Him, but it was too difficult. I couldn't leave off taking apples and things like that, or my friends would have turned against me."

"Did you leave Sunday school just because of that?" enquired Mr. White.

"There was something else, too," continued Jo. "The teacher told us that Jesus said we have to forgive our enemies. Well, I've got a cousin who's an enemy. She's horrible, and I could never leave off hating her."

Mr. White seemed deeply concerned.

"Perhaps your cousin thinks you're horrible, too," he remarked.

"She does," agreed Jo. "She hates me and she's hurt me badly, so I'm going to hurt her back."

"I think you are probably both as bad as each other," said Mr. White, looking very grave, "but the wonderful thing is that Jesus, the Good Shepherd, loves you both, and wants both of you to belong to Him."

Jo felt very sad but she did not reply.

"Could you get your cousin to come here next Sunday?" Mr. White enquired, after a pause. "If I could talk to you both together, perhaps that would help."

"Oh no," said Jo. "She's older than me and she'd never come. She hates anything like Sunday school."

"I shall be praying for you both," replied Mr. White, solemnly, "and, by the way, the boys and girls who will be arriving have their own Bibles. Have you one, too?"

"No, I've never had one of my own," said Jo.

"Well, I have a spare one here which I am going to give to you. It has quite good print and some illustrations, too."

"Oh, Mr. White, is it for my very own?" asked Jo, eagerly.

"It will belong to you and your cousin," answered Mr. White.

"But she won't want it. She'll never look at it."

"She may some day, and I want you both to share it."

"Okay. Anyway, it's super!" exclaimed Jo. "Thank you very much."

The boys and girls then started to arrive. There were twelve of them altogether, counting Jo—six boys and six girls.

One of the boys called Peter, who was fourteen, seemed to know the Bible better than anyone else, and he helped Jo find all the places. After some Bible-reading, hymns and choruses were sung, a thirteen-year-old girl called Ada accompanying them on a small piano. Then Mr. White talked to them for a while, and suggested that the class should read a few verses from the Bible every day at home.

"And I advise beginners," he said, "to read first of all, the four Gospels—Matthew, Mark, Luke and John, which tell us all about the life of Jesus Christ."

After the meeting was over, Mr. White asked Jo if she would be coming to the next one.

"Oh yes," she replied. "I shall always want to come while we are here. Aunt Bella likes this place, so I hope we won't move on yet."

On the way back to the fairground, Jo met Gloria and showed her the Bible.

"The man at the Bible class wants us to share it," she said.

"I'm not interested," answered Gloria.

"He says he wants to see you there, too. Will you come next Sunday?"

"Not likely," replied the other girl, and she hurried off without another word.

Jo went straight to the blue caravan where Granfer lived. She knew she could always be sure of a welcome there.

The old man looked thin and frail, and was half asleep in his comfortable chair. He brightened up, however, when he saw Jo, and was very interested in looking at the Bible.

"I had one and used to read it when I was your age," he said, "but I slipped up like so many young folk do. I was well educated and should have had a good job, but I got into bad company and couldn't settle down to work. In the end, I earned a hard living at circuses and travelling fairs."

"But what about your Bible?" asked Jo.

"My pals teased me out of reading it years ago, for I couldn't bear being laughed at," he replied. "I've had a difficult life, and I would have been so much happier if I had trusted in the Lord. I have come back to Him now, and I know I have been forgiven, but my sight is bad and I shall never be able to read the Bible again."

"I've got an idea," exclaimed Jo. "Mr. White has asked us to read some verses every day, so, if you like, I'll read them aloud, in your tent."

"It would be a wonderful help and comfort to me if you did," Granfer replied, gratefully.

Jo kept her promise, and every day after school she read parts of the New Testament aloud to Granfer. She also went regularly to Mr. White's Sunday class. She was learning a great deal about Jesus, and she noticed with surprise how often He spoke of His Father in heaven, and how He taught His disciples to pray to Him.

To Jo, God had always seemed remote and sometimes frightening, but Jesus taught people about His
love. He was the heavenly Father who cared even for
unimportant little sparrows, and much more for His
own children. Jo knew that she, also, could be one of
God's family and pray to Him if she came to Jesus and
asked to have her sins forgiven. It would not be at all
easy, though, she thought, for she would have to give
up doing so many things that she wanted to do.

The weeks that followed were difficult ones for her.
The fair was on nearly every night, and Jo was kept
busy behind the scenes, running errands, preparing
meals for the helpers, and washing up afterwards.
There was never any spare time now for drawing and
painting, and she was thoroughly unhappy.

One day, after she had read the tenth chapter of
John to Granfer, they talked about Jesus, the Good
Shepherd. How brave and generous He had been, Jo
thought. He had laid down His life so that everyone,
including the enemies who had hated Him, might be
forgiven, and yet *she* had refused to forgive Gloria.
She had even been frightened, too, about what her
friends would say if she became a Christian.

Later that evening, in Granfer's tent, she knelt
down and asked Jesus to come into her life and help
her to be brave and true to Him. She finished the
prayer with:

"I'm sorry I stole things and I promise not to do it
again. I won't cut up Gloria's dress after all, and I'll
try to get to like her, if you'll help me. Please forgive
me and make me one of Your own children."

A feeling of calm and security came over Jo afterwards. She knew she had a Friend now who would
understand her difficulties and be with her all her life.

When Jo came very early to the next Bible class to
tell Mr. White about her decision, he was over-joyed.
He reminded her, though, that it was not always easy

to be a Christian, and to stand up for what one believed to be right. Difficult times would be sure to come, but there was One who was in control of everything, and who would never desert her.

"I was a missionary when I was young," he added, "and often alone and sometimes frightened, but there is a verse from a well-known psalm which comforted me many times. I am going to give it to you." Then he repeated: "In His hand are all the corners of the earth: and the strength of the hills is His also."

"I like those words, too," said Jo. "I shall always remember them."

CHAPTER SEVEN

THE WILD CATS

Jo tried hard to be friendly and helpful to Gloria, but it was not easy, for the latter took little notice of her, and was with her friend, Poppy Littlewood, whenever possible.

On Friday afternoon, when passing Miss Parsons' little cottage on the way back from school, Jo suddenly remembered with a shock the row of stolen carrots. She had promised she would never again take anything that did not belong to her; but was that enough? A voice seemed to tell her that she should own up, and say she was sorry. It was never easy to own up, though, and it was especially difficult in circumstances like these. Another voice said, "Don't be silly. You might be reported to the police. It is all over now, anyway, and no one need ever know."

Jo stood hesitating at the gate. Then, suddenly, she remembered she had a Leader now who had always been honest and true, and never afraid of anything.

I must be brave too, she thought, as she walked up to the front door, her heart beating very fast. She had seen Miss Parsons peering out of a window, once, and her lined face and enormous spectacles had given Jo the impression that the old lady was very severe.

Jo forced herself to ring the bell, and then listened, with a shudder, to a tapping sound as the old lady shuffled along with the help of her two sticks.

A few seconds later the door was opened wide, and Miss Parsons exclaimed, "Bless you, my dear child! I am so thankful you have arrived."

Jo stared at her in amazement. Was she mistaking her for someone else? she wondered.

"But you tell me your business first, though," continued the old lady. "Why have you come, dear?"

"Because—because I stole your carrots," Jo blurted out.

Miss Parsons' face looked grave for a moment. "So it was you, was it, who took them?" she said. "Well, it was very wrong and it shocked me at the time, but why are you telling me this now?"

"Because I'm sorry, and I'm promising never to do things like that again."

"Then I'll forgive you, dear."

"But Miss Parsons, I—well, I haven't any money. I can't pay you back."

"True forgiveness is always free. Our Lord taught us that," said the old lady. "Do you know about Him?"

"Oh yes," answered Jo, "and I am going to try to be like Him."

"Then God bless you and keep you, my child," said Miss Parsons. "I am so grateful to you for coming," she added, "for I had been hoping all the afternoon that someone would pass this way and help me. You see, I have some very important calls to make, and my telephone is out of order. Do you think you could get to the post office before it closes, and report this for me?"

"Oh yes," said Jo, eagerly. "I'll run all the way and ask them to get it put right quickly."

Half an hour later, her errand accomplished, Jo was back on the fairground, feeling relieved and thankful.

To her surprise, Gloria came running up to her. "As it is Saturday tomorrow," she announced, "we are having a picnic party in the afternoon, and Poppy has asked you to come, too."

"But does she really want me?" Jo enquired doubtfully.

"Well, I don't suppose she would have asked you if she didn't," replied Gloria. "There will be other kids about your age, too. We are all going to meet at a gorgeous place called Cotton Grass Moor," she continued. "It's a few miles from here and on the bus route, and Mum will give us cash for our return fares. I've told Poppy you're coming."

At two o'clock the following afternoon, Gloria and Jo arrived at the appointed place where thirteen-year-old Poppy, her younger brother, and another girl called Nan and her two brothers were waiting for them.

Gloria introduced Jo to them all.

"Crumbs! You're tall, and Gloria says you can't half run," remarked Poppy's brother, Tom, admiringly. "We're the Wild Cat gang," he added. "There are six of us and you make seven."

"We've brought lots of grub with us, too," remarked one of the other boys, as they all walked together across a wide common.

"Yes, and even sugar and cream for the strawberries," said Nan.

"There's a sort of market garden near here," Poppy then explained. "The owner's away, and the place is locked up, but Gloria has found a key that fits. There are masses of strawberries there, and we are going to get some. We want you to be sentinel outside and warn us if there's anyone coming."

"But I can't do that," protested Jo.

"Of course you can," Poppy insisted. "Gloria says you run like the wind. That's why we asked you here."

"It's stealing, though," cried Jo, "and I'm not going to help you with that."

"Of course it isn't stealing," said Gloria. "It is just taking a few strawberries from someone who has got too many—and what about all those carrots that you took?"

"I know now that it was wrong, and I shan't do it any more," answered Jo.

"It's going to Bible class that's making you all smug and goodie," retorted Gloria, angrily. "If you don't help us, you won't get any tea."

"I don't want your tea. I'm going back," said Jo.

"No you aren't. Come on, Wild Cats. Let's give it to her good and strong," cried Tom, fiercely, "and take this first," he said, as he picked up a handful of earth and flung it at her face. There was some gravel with it, and Jo gave a sharp cry of pain as it grazed her forehead.

"Stop it! You're going too far!" shouted Poppy, but the three boys could no longer control their anger and excitement.

"Quick! Catch her!" they cried.

Jo dodged away from them just in time, and began running at her fastest across the common while the three boys chased after her, yelling at the tops of their voices. Their speed was no match for Jo's, though, and at last they gave up and went back, while Jo found her way to a bus stop on the main road again. She waited there for half-an-hour and then, to her relief, a bus came along and she was able to make the return journey.

Later that evening, when Gloria came back, her mother asked her if she had enjoyed herself.

"It was super," she replied.

"What's Jo been up to with that mark on 'er forehead?" Mrs. Pickleworth then enquired.

"Oh, she started fighting us," Gloria answered, carelessly. "She got the worst of it, though, and it served her right."

CHAPTER EIGHT

GLORIA IN TROUBLE

Next day, when Jo went to the Bible class as usual, Mr. White had some special news for the boys and girls.

"You have all worked so well and learnt so much about the life of our Lord that today, for a change, I have set you a competition," he said. "There are fifty questions to answer, and first and second prizes for those who get the most right."

"How smashing!" exclaimed one of the boys, "but I know Peter will win. He seems to know the four Gospels by heart."

"I wish I did," replied Peter, laughing, "but every time I learn something new, I realise how much there is left to know."

Soon the class were busy writing down their answers, and when they handed in their papers to Mr. White he told them they would have to wait till the following Sunday for the results.

There was much excitement in the little hall when the great day arrived.

"The results are very good indeed," said Mr. White, smiling. "No one has less than forty right answers, and the winner, who is Peter Blackburn, has forty-eight. Congratulations, Peter!" he added, and everyone clapped as he handed him a large volume of adventure stories.

"The winner of the second prize is a girl," continued Mr. White. "She has answered forty-five questions right, and her name is Jo Plain."

Everyone clapped again, and Jo could hardly believe her eyes when Mr. White presented her with a paint-box exactly like the one she had taken from the supermarket. She was too overcome to say a word, but she waited behind afterwards to thank him.

"It's beautiful!" she exclaimed, "and just like the one I took."

"And this time," he said, "you have earned it through your own good work. Well done!"

Jo then raced home to show the paint-box to Granfer. "Can it be kept for safety in your caravan?" she asked.

"Why, certainly," he replied, "and I shall be so pleased if you do your painting here, whenever you like. I wish Gloria would come and play her guitar to me, too, as she used to do," he remarked, sadly. "She goes out with some friends every evening, and they are not doing her any good."

The old man was right. A few nights later, the Wild Cat gang, with Gloria and Poppy as ringleaders, were caught red-handed breaking into a little shop and stealing sweets.

At almost the same time, the detective at the supermarket discovered that it was Gloria who had stolen the necklace. The latter had told her mother that Poppy's parents had given it to her, and she had been quite careless about wearing it in public. One day, she even walked into the supermarket with it on, and it so happened that the detective was in the shop that day.

Gloria had imagined that there were many other necklaces there, all exactly alike, but, unfortunately for her, the one she had taken was a sample, no longer required, and the only one of its kind.

The detective had been looking out for it for a long time, and when he saw Gloria wearing it he followed her out of the shop.

"Excuse me, young lady," he called out to her; "I want to talk to you a minute. Where did you get that necklace?"

Gloria felt a little uneasy. "My friend's dad gave it to me," she said.

"I'll have his name and address, please, and yours, too," said the detective.

Gloria, feeling really frightened now, gave him the information he wanted. There was still a good chance, though, she thought, that this matter would be overlooked.

The detective, however, wasted very little time in writing to Poppy's father, and received from him the indignant reply that he had never, on any occasion, given a necklace to Miss Gloria Pickleworth.

What happened next Gloria would have preferred to have forgotten. The visits from the police, and the endless questions which had to be answered, and the disgrace of it all, were hard for her to bear.

"What's going to happen to me?" she asked, looking terrified.

The police said that she would be tried by a juvenile court, and, after that, most likely she would be put on probation. "That means that the probation officer will keep an eye on you for a long time," they explained, "and if you misbehave again, you will probably be sent to a remand home."

Mrs. Pickleworth felt completely shattered by the news. How could Gloria, of all girls, have behaved like that, she wondered. If it had been Jo instead, she would not have been at all surprised.

"If you carry on like this, me girl," she remarked to her daughter, grimly, "you'll be landed in one of them Borstal places, an' it won't be no good yer squealing to me to get yer out."

"Oh, let's move on, Mum, and get away from it all," said Gloria.

"It won't make no difference," was the reply. "The law don't forget nothing; an' if yer break it, it just follows yer around. You'd still have to report to that there probation officer wherever yer was."

Gloria received yet another shock when a letter addressed to her mother arrived from Poppy's father. In it he wrote, 'I do not consider the friendship between our respective daughters to be at all desirable. In view of what has taken place, it is my wish that they shall no longer meet or correspond with each other.'

The last shattering blow, however, came in the postscript to the letter. It read: 'The concert in which your daughter was taking part has now been cancelled.'

Mrs. Pickleworth, worried and overwrought, seldom spoke to Jo, and, had it not been for her school work and Mr. White's Sunday classes, the girl would have felt very lonely indeed. Lessons were becoming particularly interesting just then. It seemed to Jo, too, that there was magic in the new paint-box, for the sketches which she now produced were the best she had ever done.

One day, Miss Dresden, the art mistress, spoke to her after school. "There is going to be an art exhibition at the town hall in three weeks' time," she said, "and a special competition open to anyone under eighteen years of age. The art teachers, in all the schools around, are entering their most promising pupils," she continued, "and I would very much like to put you in for it too, Jo. What do you say about that?"

"Oh, Miss Dresden, would I be good enough?" asked Jo.

"I think you would," replied the art mistress. "I have been more than satisfied with the sketches you have been handing in to me lately. In the competition you have to show four water-colour paintings, and you can use your imagination and choose any subjects you like. The special prize for the best four pictures is five pounds, but there will be a number of book prizes, too, to encourage younger competitors like you. It would be such good practice for you."

"I'd like to try ever so much," cried Jo. "I don't know whether my aunt would let me, though."

"Well, please tell her, anyway, that there will be no question of expense," replied Miss Dresden. "It will be a pleasure to me to pay for the few extra materials you will need, such as drawing paper and cardboard on which to mount the pictures."

"Oh, thank you, Miss Dresden! I'll try my best to enter," said Jo.

"There is just one other thing to tell you," added Miss Dresden. "Nearly all the paintings shown will be the work of young people; but we are really very fortunate, for Mr. John Trevellian is paying us a visit that day, and has agreed to exhibit some of his pictures."

"Is he a real artist?" asked Jo, eagerly.

"He most certainly is—one of the best known in our country. His pictures are so beautiful, too. I think you will learn quite a lot just from looking at them."

"A real artist!" Jo whispered to herself as she left the school. "Now I shall be able to find out what artists are really like."

As she walked back to the fairground, however, she began to feel afraid that neither Gloria nor her mother would want her to take part in the painting competition. What could she do about it, then? Suddenly she had an idea. Gloria was always wanting money. So she would tell her about the first prize of five pounds which was being offered.

"I'll try ever so hard to win it," she said to Gloria, a few minutes later, "and if I do, I'll share it with you."

"You mean you'd give me two pounds fifty out of it?"

"Of course I would."

"Crumbs! I could do with it. I want some ear-rings and a necklace something like the one I had to give back, and lots of other things," remarked Gloria. "Do you think you could win it, though?"

"I don't know," answered Jo. "There will be crowds of people older than me trying, but I'd do my very best, I promise."

"Okay, then. I'll explain to Mum how clumsy you are at the fair, and I'll say you'd be much better out of the way, doing this painting."

"You see, Mum, I really don't want her dropping things and knocking them about," Gloria remarked to her mother later that evening.

Mrs. Pickleworth's attitude towards her unhappy daughter was beginning to soften. "All right, pet," she replied. "Them stupid pictures'll keep 'er quiet an' out of mischief."

The next three weeks were the happiest and the most satisfying that Jo could remember. Every afternoon, as soon as her school work was finished, she went to the blue caravan and settled down there to paint her pictures. Granfer's table was just the right height for her, and Miss Dresden had provided all the materials needed.

Granfer very much enjoyed watching the pictures develop. The first one was of the fairground, and all the brightly coloured caravans, including Granfer's, were shown in it.

The second one was of Gloria, in her best crimson dress, with Cocky perched on her shoulder. Then, in the third one, Jo painted the three little dogs, Salt, Pepper and Mustard. Each was riding a Shetland pony, as they had done so often in the past.

It was Jo's fourth picture, though, which Granfer thought the best. In it she painted, from memory, the lions and bears which had also performed at the circus.

"My word!" exclaimed the old man. "You are making those beasts come alive, and I'm getting quite scared of them!"

CHAPTER NINE

JO MEETS AN ARTIST

The art exhibition took place on a Saturday, and all the competitors were asked to put their paintings in the big hall between eight and ten o'clock that morning.

Mrs. Pickleworth insisted that Jo should do her share of washing up and cleaning before she left, and so it was nearly ten o'clock when she arrived at the hall. All the other competitors had arranged their paintings and left. The hall was empty except for a young man, acting as steward, who was seated at a table at the far end. He got up when he saw Jo, and showed her where to fix her pictures. He told her that the panel of judges would be arriving at eleven o'clock. The hall would then be closed to the general public until two thirty, when the exhibition would be open.

"The prizes will be distributed early," he added, "as some of the young folk have come a long distance, and will have to start home again."

Jo felt quite bewildered as she walked round, for the walls were covered with paintings of every description.

"Mr. John Trevellian's pictures are near the door on the right," the steward called out to her, as he walked back to his place at the table.

Jo gasped with wonder and surprise as she looked at them. Never in her life had she seen such beautiful paintings. Many of them were of people and animals, but much more 'real and alive' than her own, she thought.

There were pictures, too, of purple moors and peaceful gardens, and of stormy seas with black thunderclouds riding above them. The painting which delighted Jo most of all, though, was of a clearing in a wood where a little stream wound its way among the trees. The whole scene was aglow with a most wonderful sunset, and the shafts of light were shining on two deer which had come to the water's edge to drink.

"Coo!" exclaimed Jo. "If I could paint like that!"

Suddenly she noticed that an old man had entered the hall. His hair was rather long and untidy, and his jacket shabby and thin at the elbows. This must be the artist, then, she thought. Gloria was right after all, for they did dress like that. What did it matter, though, when they painted such beautiful pictures?

She went straight up to him. "Excuse me," she said, "but I think your pictures are smashing."

"Pretty good show this year," he agreed.

"But how do you manage to paint such super ones?"

He looked at her in amusement. "I paint them!" he chuckled. "I'm no artist. I'm the cleaner and caretaker here."

"Oh, I'm sorry. I—I didn't know," stammered Jo, feeling very embarrassed. "But where is the artist?"

"He'll be about somewhere," was the reply. "He's not an old fogey like me. You must look out for a chap in his forties. Very tall he is, too, and smart-looking. He did say he had to go to the picture shop at the top of the hill. Maybe he's still there."

"Thank you," said Jo. "Oh dear!" she muttered under her breath. "I'll have to find him somehow."

She hurried up the long hill to the art shop, but when she burst in there was no one there except a fair-haired girl who was standing behind the counter.

"Please, where's the artist?" Jo asked.

"Don't know who you mean," was the reply. "There was a gentleman here half an hour ago who mentioned he was going to an art exhibition, if that's any help."

"Yes, that's who I mean," Jo replied. "I'll have to go back and look for him again."

As she drew near the town hall she saw, to her relief, a tall man with brown wavy hair that was turning a little grey. He had just come out of the main entrance, and sat down on a seat in the sun. He was wearing a well-tailored suit, and he seemed to fit the caretaker's description of the artist.

"Excuse me," Jo said, rather hesitatingly this time, "but you are, aren't you—I mean—I think your pictures are super!"

The tall man fixed his large brown eyes on her. "I am glad you like them," he replied quietly.

"The one with the deer by the stream is the one I like best," continued Jo. "The sunset is absolutely perfect. How did you get all the right colours?"

"I did my best," Mr. Trevellian answered, "but it is far from perfect. Only the greatest Artist of all can paint a sunset. Do you know who I mean?"

"Oh yes, you mean God, the heavenly Father," said Jo. "I've learnt about Him. I know about Jesus, the Good Shepherd, too, and I have asked Him to come into my life."

"I am so glad you have," replied the artist, a smile lighting up his kind face. "I am waiting for my sister," he explained. "She and I have just had a very quick preview of the paintings. Come and sit here, too, if you like. The greatest Artist of all is also the Creator of everything, isn't He?" he added, thoughtfully, as Jo sat down beside him.

"Yes," agreed Jo, "and the minister at the Bible class where I go gave me a verse to learn about Him. It's this: 'In His hand are all the corners of the earth: and the strength of the hills is His also.'"

"Well remembered," said the artist, "and the next part is: 'The sea is His, and He made it: And His hands prepared the dry land.'"

"Then you know it, too!" exclaimed Jo, in surprise.

"Yes, it is the ninety-fifth psalm, and my sister and I sing it in our church every Sunday morning."

"Does your sister live with you?" asked Jo.

"Yes, she does, I am glad to say. She is a bit older than I am, and she keeps me in order."

"Oh!" cried Jo, as a sudden idea came into her head. "Do you keep her?"

"What do you mean by that?"

"I mean, do you pay for her food and everything yourself?"

"Why yes, of course. That's the least I can do, isn't it, when she is so kind to me?" answered Mr. Trevellian, looking rather surprised.

"Do you mind if I ask you another personal question?" continued Jo.

"No. Fire away," he replied, trying to hide a smile.

"Well, are the clothes you are wearing your own?"

"You don't think I stole them, do you?" he asked, pretending to be shocked.

"Oh, no, of course I don't," said Jo. "I just wondered if, perhaps, you had borrowed them."

Mr. Trevellian was now finding it very difficult not to laugh outright.

"They were made to measure," he answered as seriously as he could. "Don't you think they fit me properly?"

"Oh yes, they're quite all right. I just wanted to know, that's all."

"Now look here," said the artist, "don't you think it's my turn now to ask you a question?"

"That's fair enough," she agreed.

"Well, I would like to know, please, why you are asking me so many things."

"It's because of Gloria," replied Jo. "She's my cousin, and she said artists never had any money, and the clothes they wore were all borrowed. I wanted to show her she was wrong."

"Well," said Mr. Trevellian, "you can tell Miss Gloria that I am quite comfortably off, thank you, with a house and a car, and I don't need to borrow money or clothes or anything. Of course," he added, "artists do sometimes go through hard times until they become well-known, but so do authors and musicians and many other people. I still don't understand why you are so interested in how artists live, though."

"It's because I want to be one myself," Jo announced.

"Do you really?" asked Mr. Trevellian, looking still more surprised.

"Yes, I want to, more than anything else in the world. Do you think I ever will be?"

"It is difficult to say," answered Mr. Trevellian, seriously. "If you have a bit of talent in that direction, and work very hard, I dare say it is possible." Then, noticing the girl's anxious face, he added, "It is surprising what young people can sometimes do. There's a boy showing the most amazing pictures at this exhibition today. He's a born artist, and only twelve years old."

"But I didn't notice his paintings," exclaimed Jo, feeling very puzzled indeed. "Whereabouts are they?"

"I'll show them to you as my sister still hasn't arrived," said Mr. Trevellian.

They went back into the hall together, and then, to Jo's astonishment, he led her to where her own pictures were.

"There," he said. "You wouldn't believe a young lad could do such beautiful work, would you?"

"But he didn't!" cried Jo. "I'm Jo Plain, and I painted them."

Mr. Trevellian looked at her in astonishment. "I

think there is a mistake here," he answered. "Anyway, you must be older than this young competitor."

"But I'm not. I'm only twelve," insisted Jo, "and I can't help growing so tall."

At that moment, Mr. Trevellian's sister arrived. She was very like her brother in appearance, but plumper and not so tall.

"Mary!" exclaimed the artist, "this girl says she is Jo, and it is she who has painted these wonderful pictures."

"Congratulations, my dear," said Miss Trevellian, shaking hands with Jo. "I'm glad we've met. Your pictures really are lovely. I am wondering, too, what gave you the idea of painting a fairground and so many delightful animals."

"We've got a travelling fair," Jo replied.

"You mean your father and mother run one?"

"No, they are both dead, but my aunt does, and she looks after me."

"It must be very exciting, travelling from place to place," the artist broke in.

"It isn't really," replied Jo. "I hate it."

Mr. Trevellian and his sister looked surprised. "But why?" they asked.

"Because I'm so tired of moving on and on, and I'm no good at helping with the fair."

"There is so much I would like to ask you about your painting," said Mr. Trevellian, "but I don't think we are meant to loiter here. Let's sit out in the sun again, shall we?"

He led the way to the seat outside.

"My dad was a sort of artist, too," remarked Jo, as they all sat down together.

"Was he indeed?" said Mr. Trevellian, looking interested. "What did he do?"

"He was a trapeze artist," replied Jo, "and he did all sorts of things on a tight rope."

"Then he must have been very clever indeed," replied Mr. Trevellian, smiling.

Jo turned then to the artist's sister. "I'm sorry, I can't remember your name," she said.

"It's Trevellian, dear, but it is rather long and difficult to say. What about calling us just Uncle John and Auntie Mary?"

"I'd like to," agreed Jo, "and I wish you were my real aunt and uncle, but, Miss Trer—Trer—I mean Auntie, I must tell you all the funny things Cocky, the macaw in my picture, says."

Then Jo was soon describing not only Cocky, but all the other pets, and giving an account of what she, herself, did each day. Usually she was shy with strangers, but these new friends were very kind and understanding, and it was so easy to talk to them.

"Have you really never had any lessons in drawing and painting, except a few at different schools, as you have travelled about?" asked Mr. Trevellian at last.

"No," said Jo. "You see, Aunt Bella thinks drawing is a waste of time, and, Mr. Trer—I mean Uncle, I have been praying for something for such a long time. Do you think it could be too difficult for God to make it happen?"

"Nothing is too hard for God to do," said the artist. "He always answers prayer; but, often, not just as we ask Him, but in the way He knows to be best. We have to learn to be patient, and sometimes wait a long time for anything to happen."

"Well, I don't want to clean out caravans all my life," replied Jo. "I want to have lots of time for drawing and painting, and plenty of lessons, too, to help me to get better. I don't see how it can ever happen, though. It seems impossible."

"Jo, dear," broke in Miss Trevellian. "When I was your age and difficulties sometimes came, an old friend of mine used to tell me that, if I trusted in God, He would make a way for me through them, and I found this was always true. She told me the story—perhaps you know it already—of the Israelites starting on their journey to the Promised Land. They were soon in fearful danger with the enemy army of the Egyptians chasing them from behind, and with nothing but the Red Sea in front of them. There seemed no possibility of escape."

"Yes, I remember that Bible story," said Jo. "The minister read it to us out of the Book of Exodus. The Israelites prayed to God in their danger, didn't they, and he made a strong wind blow. The waters went back, and there was a path across the sea and they got safely over."

"Yes, and He will make a path for us, too, through all our difficulties, if we trust Him," said Miss Trevellian.

"Never lose faith then, Jo," the artist added, "and never leave off praying. I feel sure God gave you that talent for a purpose, and some day He means you to use it. Life is not always meant to be easy, though, for any of us. My sister and I have had a great deal of trouble, but God has helped us through it. Remember, too, won't you, that Jesus, God's Son, loved us so much that He came down into this world to help and to heal, and to die for us."

"Yes," said Jo. "Thank you for telling me, and I'm glad I met you. I think I'd better go now, or everyone will be wondering what's happened to me. I shall be back at half past two, though, and I'm allowed to stay till six o'clock, when I can take down my paintings and bring them back. Shall I see you both again at the exhibition?" she asked, anxiously.

"Of course you will," they replied. "We are staying at the Swan Hotel, which is quite near it. What about your coming to tea with us afterwards?"

"That would be super!" exclaimed Jo. "Thank you very much. Goodbye, Auntie and Uncle."

The next moment she was hurrying back to the fairground, where she soon found Gloria.

"I've seen a real artist," she cried, "and he's got lots of money and a house and a car and a nice suit, which he bought himself and——"

"Well, you've struck lucky, then," interrupted Gloria. "There aren't many like that. Poppy said all the ones she knew hadn't got a bean."

CHAPTER TEN

THE ART EXHIBITION

It was long after half past two, and the exhibition had been open some time when Jo arrived, hot and out of breath. The three dogs had taken it into their heads to go rabbit hunting that afternoon, and it was she who had to find them and bring them back.

The hall was very full, and as she squeezed her way in she noticed three men facing her behind a table at the far end. They were standing on a platform which was decorated with a number of enormous earthenware jars filled with foxgloves and ferns.

As she entered, she heard one of the men remark, "We have now distributed all the books, and no doubt you can hardly wait to know who has won the prize for the best paintings of the exhibition. I will not keep you in suspense. It has been awarded to twelve-year-old Jo Plain for work of outstanding quality and charm.

"Jo, will you please come up and receive your prize."

As Jo walked forward she felt she was in a dream. She could only move very slowly through the crowd, and the voice from the platform started calling out again. "Is Jo Plain here this afternoon?"

"Yes, I am trying to come," she replied, in a small, frightened voice.

People then turned round and smiled, and made way for her. She soon reached the platform and climbed up the steps to it. Then an elderly gentleman in glasses, after congratulating her, handed her a certificate, and the prize money in an envelope.

Everyone clapped loudly as she turned round to climb down, but in her excitement she forgot to notice where she was walking. The next moment, to her horror, she had kicked over one of the enormous earthenware jars, and there seemed to be water running everywhere.

"Oh crumbs! I'm sorry. What shall I do?" she exclaimed, her face turning scarlet.

"Don't you worry, my dear," said the kind old gentleman. "Worse things than that happen at sea. You just think of the pleasure you will give us one day, when we hope to see your pictures hanging in the Royal Academy."

Jo came down the steps carefully, while everyone clapped again. Then, as the water dripped down from the platform to the floor beneath, a row of teenagers sitting near, grateful to her, perhaps, for bringing a little variety into the programme, started cheering her, and singing, "For she's a jolly good fellow."

Feeling still more embarrassed, Jo hurried to the door marked 'Exit', while people patted her on the back as she passed them. At last she was safely outside the hall, and, almost immediately afterwards, Mr. Trevellian and his sister joined her.

"Well done, dear!" they exclaimed. "We are so proud of our new niece. What a splendid result!"

"But did you see what I did?" said Jo. "I made a flood on the platform. It was awful."

"Don't let that bother you," said Mr. Trevellian. "I upset things, too, and my sister is always mopping up after me. Won't you come back into the hall, though? Everyone will want to talk to you and congratulate you."

"Oh, no," said Jo. "I've had enough."

"Well, what about a motor drive with us, and tea in the hotel garden afterwards?"

"That would be gorgeous," replied Jo. "I'll be as quick as I can, but I'll have to go and see Gloria first, and give her two pound fifty. You see, I promised to share my prize with her."

"But that was most kind and generous!" exclaimed Miss Trevellian.

"It wasn't really," said Jo, feeling a bit guilty. "I promised her that because I knew I wouldn't be allowed to go to the exhibition if I didn't."

"May I see your certificate, Jo, before you go?" asked the artist.

"Of course, Uncle John," replied Jo, handing it to him. "I shan't want it back again."

"But you ought to keep it," said Mr. Trevellian.

"I've nowhere to put it, and it will get spoilt in the tent, so you have it if you like," she replied.

As she hurried away, the artist called out to her, "We shall be waiting for you in the garden of the Swan Hotel."

"What a dear child she is!" Miss Trevellian remarked to her brother. "Those deep blue eyes and long dark eyelashes——" she continued thoughtfully. "Do you know, John, she'll be a beautiful woman one day, too, when she gets over the awkward, growing stage."

"And you'll have to wait a long time for that to happen," answered her brother, "for, incredible though it may seem, that child is only twelve years old. There are plenty of art students, twice her age too, who would give a great deal to possess that amazing natural talent."

Jo, meanwhile, was hurrying back to the fairground, where Gloria was waiting anxiously.

"Gloria! I've got it! A five-pound note," she called out as she arrived.

"Good for you!" exclaimed Gloria, "And you've really promised, haven't you?"

"Of course," said Jo, "but the note will have to be changed first."

At that moment, Mrs. Pickleworth came out of her caravan.

"Mum!" exclaimed Gloria, "Jo's won five pounds for her pictures!"

"Oh my!" said Mrs. Pickleworth. "Fancy that, now! I wouldn't have thought them worth it."

"She's letting me have half the money, so please can you give us two pounds fifty each," continued Gloria.

Mrs. Pickleworth took the note and went into her caravan. She came out again almost at once, and handed each of the girls fifty pence. "There," she said, "you can have this, but I'll need to take the rest for yer keep."

"But it's my prize money," cried Jo indignantly. "I won it."

"Yes, it *is* hers," agreed Gloria, "and she promised to give me half."

"An' who puts clothes on yer backs, I ask yer, an' shoe leather on yer feet, an' who feeds yer, too, an' both eatin' like 'orses?" asked Mrs. Pickleworth, crossly. "I've given yer fifty pence each to fritter away, an' if that ain't fair an' proper I'd like to know what is."

"It ain't fair and it ain't proper, neither," shouted Gloria, forgetting in her agitation all the good grammar she had learnt at school. She began to cry aloud, and tears of disappointment were also streaming down Jo's cheeks.

"You get out of my sight, you couple of squalling brats, or I'll take away what I've given yer," cried Mrs. Pickleworth, angrily.

Gloria went into her tent and lay on her back for a while, kicking and screaming, while Jo ran quickly to Granfer's caravan.

"My poor little maid!" exclaimed the old man, noticing her tearful face. "You didn't win a prize, then, but one can't always be lucky, you know."

"But I did win a prize," said Jo. "I won the five pounds, and Aunt Bella's taken nearly all of it. I wanted to buy books about painting, and all sorts of things, and it's not fair."

"I'm sorry," said Granfer, "but don't think too badly of Bella. She was brought up the hard way, and never had a penny to throw about when she was a kid. I'd like to give you some cash myself," he added, "but I've handed over my pension to Bella. because I can't be bothered with it now. I'll say this for her: she's good to me, and buys me all I need—doesn't even forget my papers and my little bag of peppermints for Sunday. Cheer up, love," he added. "You'll grow up pretty soon and then you'll earn money to buy what you want."

Jo had already wiped her eyes, for a happy thought had struck her. "Oh, Granfer!" she exclaimed. "I've remembered I must get tidy quickly, for I'm going out to tea with a real artist and his sister."

The Trevellians were both looking out for Jo when she arrived at the Swan Hotel, and she soon explained to them what had happened.

"It is such a shame," Miss Trevellian remarked. "Jo really does deserve a good prize. Don't you think we could give her one, John?"

"No, thank you," said Jo, quietly. "It's so kind of you, but Aunt Bella wouldn't let me keep it."

"Well, could I call on your aunt," suggested the artist, "and see if she will allow you to go to a special school where art would be taught and encouraged?"

"Oh, no," answered Jo, looking frightened. "Please don't do that. She'd be mad with me, and she would never let me go."

"We would so like to do something to help you, dear," said Miss Trevellian, thoughtfully.

"I have another idea," her brother remarked, suddenly. "We shall be staying here about eight weeks. Have you any afternoons when you are free, Jo?"

"Yes, always on Mondays," she replied. "The fair

doesn't run that day, and we are allowed to do what we like after school."

"Well, while we are here, would you like to spend as much of that afternoon as possible with us each week, and do some drawing and painting with me?"

"You mean you would give me some lessons?" asked Jo, eagerly.

"Certainly I would, and I daresay you would also teach me a thing or two," said the artist.

"Oh, no, I could never do that, but it would be absolutely gorgeous to learn with you," she exclaimed, clapping her hands.

"Well, that's settled then," he replied. "The day after tomorrow is Monday, and we shall expect you as soon after school as you can manage."

"And now for a nice motor drive," suggested his sister, "and we've ordered strawberries and cream with our tea in the garden later."

On the following Monday afternoon, Mr. Trevellian waited a long time for his pupil to come. "Whatever can have happened to her?" he asked his sister.

Then suddenly Jo arrived, hot, untidy and out of breath, and carrying something wrapped up in a coat.

Miss Trevellian's sharp eyes noticed that the girl had been crying. "What's the matter, dear?" she asked anxiously.

"I can't come after all," panted Jo. "We are moving on, and I'm so disappointed."

"So are we," said the artist. "Where are you going?"

"I don't know. Aunt Bella never tells us beforehand. I'm supposed to be helping to pack up, but I had to come and say goodbye to you."

"My dear child," replied Miss Trevellian. "I do so wish we could do something to help you."

"At any rate, you must have our home address," said the artist, "and if ever you are in our direction, we hope you will come and see us. We live in a little town called Rosewell, twenty miles from the big market town of Oxenmead. There," he continued, "I've written the address down for you."

"Thank you," said Jo, taking the slip of paper which he handed her. "I mustn't stay, or I'll get into a row."

She gave Miss Trevellian a quick hug, and shook hands with her brother. "Thank you both for everything," she said, "and I do wish I didn't have to leave you. Oh, and I was nearly forgetting something," she added, as she unwrapped the coat she was carrying, and took out from it her four exhibition paintings. "These are for you," she said, as she thrust two of the pictures into Mr. Trevellian's arms, and two into his sister's. Then, without waiting to be thanked, she ran off.

Miss Trevellian watched her go, with tears in her eyes. "Oh, John," she cried, "she came into our life so suddenly, and now she has gone out of it again, and we can't do anything for her! The situation seems hopeless."

"No situation is beyond our Lord's control," her brother answered quietly. "That child knows about the Good Shepherd. She is one of His own, and He will never desert her."

CHAPTER ELEVEN

A SHOCK FOR JO

Jo found it difficult to settle down at the new fairground, outside the small town of Oakvale. She had had only a few minutes to say goodbye to Mr. White, and to Miss Dresden, the art mistress, and she was bitterly disappointed, too, at not being able to see any more of the Trevellians.

At her new school, however, her form mistress, Miss Bell, a kindly middle-aged woman, seemed most understanding.

"I'm sure everything must seem a bit strange to you at first," she remarked, when Jo arrived.

"I'm missing my friends so much," Jo replied. "We've come from Swanford. How far is it from here, please?"

"A good eighty miles, I should think," replied Miss Bell.

"And I've got other friends whose home is at Rosewell," she continued, thinking of the Trevellians. "How far away would that be?"

"I am afraid I don't know where Rosewell is," Miss Bell confessed.

"It is twenty miles from Oxenmead, a big market town," answered Jo, remembering what the artist had told her.

"Oh, Oxenmead, yes, I have been there once," said Miss Bell. "You go first through Newford Gorse, which is quite forty miles away. I should think Oxenmead, then, would be about a hundred miles from here. I am afraid your friends are quite out of reach at present," she added, "but I hope you will make some new ones. A friend of mine runs a youth club on Wednesday evenings. Would you like to join it?"

"My aunt doesn't allow me to go out in the evening," replied Jo.

"I have a Bible class every Sunday afternoon for girls of your age. What about coming to that, then?"

"Yes, I'd like to," Jo agreed.

Gloria, unlike Jo, settled down very quickly at Oakvale, her only annoyance being that she had to attend school regularly. As expected, she had been tried by a juvenile court, and now, with the eyes of a probation officer still on her, she felt she must be on her best behaviour.

Soon after the fair left Swanford, Granfer's health began to fail, and both Jo and Gloria were distressed to see him becoming so much weaker. Jo continued to read him a passage from the Bible each day, and she sat with him as long as she was allowed. Gloria visited him frequently also, but never at the same time as Jo.

One Sunday afternoon, after returning from the Bible class, Jo told him that Miss Bell had read aloud some verses from the first chapter of John's Gospel. "They were about Andrew who found Jesus and then brought his brother to Him," she explained. "Miss Bell told us we should all be like Andrew and bring other people to Him," she continued, "but it's no good about Gloria. She'll never come."

"We must pray that she will one day," replied the old man.

"She'd make a super Andrew and bring lots of other people, if she did," said Jo, "for all her friends, and even Aunt Bella, too, nearly always take her advice, and do exactly what she says."

"Yes, young Gloria has a will of her own," answered Granfer, smiling. "Pray God she will one day use it in the right direction."

The two girls were walking to school one morning when Gloria announced that she had made a new friend called Laura. "She's older than Poppy, and she is allowed to drive a car," she remarked. "She got interested in me because I play the guitar much better than she does, though she has had lots of lessons. I'm helping her with it, and guess what's happening later?"

"I haven't a clue," said Jo.

"Well, there's going to be a sort of music festival in the autumn, and Laura and I are going to enter for it, playing the guitars and singing."

"Is there a prize for it?" asked Jo.

"Yes, there's a silver cup, and everyone's sure I'll win it, and I'd like Laura to come second, if possible. There's something else happening much sooner, though. You guess again."

"But I can't," said Jo. "You'd better tell me."

"Well, Mum wants to make a good impression in this new place, so we're having another concert in the big marquee one Saturday evening soon, and I'll be singing and dancing on the platform again. I just can't wait for it to happen."

Gloria felt still more excited on the day of the concert. In the afternoon, she persuaded her mother to take her to the shops to buy her a new pair of dancing shoes.

Jo was glad she was allowed to remain on the fairground and look after the animals and birds. When she went round to look at Cocky, she found him perched in a corner of his enormous cage, with his back to her.

"Cocky, what's the matter with you?" she cried. "Don't look so dismal. You are going to be in a show tonight."

Cocky, however, paid no attention to her, and his eyes appeared to be closed.

"Oh dear, I'll have to find some nice nuts to cheer you up," she exclaimed.

She hurried into the pets' caravan, forgetting that

she had left the cage door off the fastener. Unfortunately for her, Cocky was not nearly as sleepy as he appeared. There was a sudden flapping of wings and the sound of the cage door springing back, and the next moment, with a raucous shriek, he alighted on the roof of the caravan.

"Oh, Cocky!" exclaimed Jo, in dismay. "Please come back. Cocky! Cocky!"

"Evening piper! Evening piper!" he called out, as he flew from one caravan roof to another.

In despair, Jo rushed off to find Dick Rogers. "I let Cocky out by mistake," she cried. "Oh please, please get him in again."

"I'll do my best, Jo, but it won't be easy," he replied. "Poor kid!" he whispered to his wife. "She'll catch it if that bird's not back in time for the show."

Dick came along as quickly as possible, carrying a pair of steps under one arm, and some slices of apple to tempt the bird in his other hand.

Cocky was now sun-bathing on the top of the marquee, and he watched with great interest as Dick climbed the steps. Then, without even waiting for the apple to be offered to him, he flew away suddenly, his great wings spread out and his blue and gold plumage flashing in the sunlight. "Have a cup of tea. Happy Christmas, dear!" he called out, as he made his way towards some woods.

"No good going after him," Dick remarked, "but, as sure as eggs is eggs, he'll be back again before dark."

"But the show starts early," said Jo, in despair.

"I know," answered Dick, sympathetically, "but don't fret too much, there's a good lass. It was an accident."

When Gloria came back and heard the news, she flew into a temper.

"I'm terribly sorry. I really am," Jo told her.

"You're not a bit. You did it on purpose," was the

reply. "You told me once you were going to pay me out. You are mean and horrible and I hate you."

Mrs. Pickleworth was even more upset, and in the heat of the moment said many things to Jo which she regretted afterwards. "You've been nothing but a trouble to me," she complained. "I don't know why I ever took you in. You're not one of us."

"But I'm your niece," said Jo. "My mother was your sister."

"You're no niece of mine," continued Mrs. Pickleworth, angrily. "I don't know who yer mother was. I just know that she died. That's all. An' I took yer in, an' this is the way you've paid me back."

"But you told me your sister was killed in a motor accident," said Jo, turning very white.

"Well, I told yer a pack of lies, because it suited me; an' now it don't suit me no more, so I'm telling yer the truth."

"But my mother?" Jo implored. "Please tell me what happened to her."

"She was drowned, an' yer was brought to me alive. I thought it best not to be told where you'd come from, as I didn't want no trouble with the police. That's all I know, an' it's the truth. Now go away or yer'll drive me up the wall."

"But there must be someone who knows what happened. Please, please tell me who does," begged Jo, and, in her desperation, she caught hold of Mrs. Pickleworth's arm and clung to it tightly.

"There's only one person in the world who knows," said Mrs. Pickleworth, trying to free her arm from the girl's grip. "You'd better get 'im to tell yer."

"But who?" asked Jo, wildly.

"It's Granfer."

"Granfer?" repeated Jo, in astonishment.

"Yes, 'e knows because 'e brought yer to me."

CHAPTER TWELVE

GRANFER'S SECRET

Granfer was lying back in his chair, his eyes closed, when Jo burst into his caravan.

"Oh, Granfer!" she exclaimed. "Aunt Bella says she's not my real aunt, and you can tell me everything."

The old man sat up quickly, and for a moment looked confused and troubled. Then, suddenly, a calm, happy expression came over his face. "Did Bella really say so?" he asked. "All these years I have wanted to tell you, but I had made a promise to her to keep it secret, and I could not break my word."

"But Granfer, please, what happened?"

"I was the only witness of a very sad accident," he replied, "and, to my sin and shame, I was not brave enough to report it."

"Please go on, Granfer."

"Well, it was about twelve years ago, though it does seem more like a hundred years now. We were camping then near the beach of a seaside village. The coast was wild and rugged looking, and I can still remember a cliff path. It was used as a short cut from the houses near the beach to a road where some shops were."

"The fair was moving on that night," Granfer continued slowly, "and I was coming back from the shops late in the afternoon. It was cold and misty, too, but I could just see a young woman pushing a pram along the cliff path in front of me. Maybe she had been shopping, too, and was getting back to her home. I think she turned round and saw me, so I whistled to show I was friendly and didn't mean her any harm. She started walking faster, though, so I kept well back as I didn't want to scare her. Then, all at once, the mist turned into a real blanket of fog, as it does sometimes in those parts."

Granfer hesitated.

"Please tell me the rest," said Jo, her voice shaking. "I want to know everything."

"Well, suddenly I heard someone call out, and the next moment I knew the poor lady had fallen over the cliff. I wanted to try and save her, but I couldn't see one step in front of me. When at last the fog cleared, I knew it was too late, and, anyway, I couldn't get down that steep cliff with the sea below."

"What did you do then?" asked Jo.

"I looked round, and I suddenly saw the pram turned over on the edge of the cliff," said Granfer, "and I heard a little cry near it, and there, fallen out of it, and all among the blankets and pillows, was a baby girl."

"And that was me," whispered Jo, her face as white as chalk.

"Yes," said Granfer, "and then I did a wicked thing that's haunted me for years."

"But what did you do that was so bad?" asked Jo.

"Well, I thought if I told the police the truth they would never believe me. They'd think I'd pushed the lady into the sea, and I'd be jailed for life. There was no one about, and I was so scared, and I suddenly had the idea that if the pram was in the sea, too, it would look like the real accident it really was. Without even stopping to think, I put the things back in it and pushed it over the cliff. Then I carried you away as quickly as I could, wrapped up in a blanket which I kept for you."

"But, Granfer, was my mother really drowned? Are you sure?"

"Yes, my dear. I read in the paper soon afterwards that her body was recovered from the sea."

"Oh," said Jo gravely, "but, Granfer, wasn't there anyone else with my mother?"

"No, the poor lady was all alone."

"And what happened to me next?"

"I gave you to Bella because she had only one child, and she wanted a playmate for Gloria. She took you in and cared for you, but she thought it best to ask no questions about you, for she was as scared as I was of the police. That night we travelled a long, long distance away. Well, that's the whole story, and, now you know it, can you ever forgive me?" he asked anxiously.

Jo slipped a hand into one of his. "But, Granfer, you saved my life," she said. "I would have died of cold and hunger, or perhaps rolled over the cliff before anyone found me."

"That may be true. It was a bitter night," replied Granfer, as he lay back in his chair, now completely exhausted.

"But where did it happen?" asked Jo. "Please tell me the name of the place."

"I don't know. I've forgotten," said the old man, closing his eyes. "So many places and so much moving on," he added, wearily.

Jo sat beside him in silence and bewilderment, her heart beating very fast. Surely this must be a dream from which she must soon awaken—but no, it was all true, and everything was different now. It was so strange and frightening.

At last Granfer made an effort to arouse himself. "Jo," he said suddenly, "I am going to advise you to do something which may shock you. I think you should run away."

"Granfer!" exclaimed Jo, in astonishment.

"I know," he continued, "that it is stupid and wrong for most young people to leave their homes, and many parents' hearts have been broken because they have done so, but it is different for you. You see, you don't belong here, and you would be happier somewhere else, I think. You should go to one of your teachers, or to a minister and tell him what has happened."

"But I couldn't," cried Jo, looking terrified. "No one would believe me, and I would be sent back. Besides, Aunt Bella (I'll still call her that) is giving up the fair soon. She says she is going to live in Yorkshire. I expect I'll be happier then, and, anyway, I think I ought to stay with her."

"But she is not taking you with her, my poor little lass," said Granfer. "She told me she wouldn't have room for you, and would be finding some other place where you could go."

"Not taking me!" Tears of indignation and self-pity came into Jo's eyes, and she tried to blink them back. "Anyway, Granfer, I'm never leaving you. I couldn't bear it," she added.

The old man was thoughtful for a few minutes. "Well, love," he said at last, "Bella has been good to me, and I'm pretty sure she won't desert me as long as I am here. As you know, though, I am expecting to be called home any time now, and I am ready and willing to go. When that happy day has come for me, you watch what Bella does; and if she starts packing up and selling her stock, take my advice and get away quickly."

"Oh, Granfer!" was all Jo could say, and again she struggled to keep back the tears.

"Now cheer up, love. I've got something for you," he said, "and it is something I never thought to have had, as it's yours already."

"What do you mean?" asked Jo.

Granfer drew from his waistcoat pocket a small, tarnished silver rattle, with a bone ring attached to it and some little silver bells.

"Crumbs!" exclaimed Jo, taking it from him. "Whatever is it?"

"It's a baby's rattle," Granfer explained, "and it fell

out of the pram that day when I found you. It was wrong of me, but I kept it because it's made of silver. I thought I'd sell it. No one would give me the price I wanted for it, though, and I am very glad now they didn't, and I can return it to you."

"But I don't want it, thank you, Granfer. What would I do with a baby's rattle?"

"You might need to sell it one day, so you hide it away where Miss Gloria's bright black eyes won't spy it. She'd soon find a way to change it into more necklaces and ear-rings."

"Okay, I'll keep it in my safest pocket, and now I'd better go. And Granfer," she added, giving him a hug, "thank you for rescuing me from that awful cliff."

Jo went straight to the macaw's cage, and was very much relieved to find that Cocky had flown home again and was none the worse for his adventure. She realised sadly, though, that the concert, by that time, was nearly over, and that Gloria must have appeared on the stage without the bird.

As she entered her tent, she noticed that all Gloria's bedding had been moved out again. She was glad to be alone that night, however. She was feeling tired out and very unhappy, and the words, 'You don't belong here', kept haunting her all the time. She did not feel she belonged anywhere now, and this was so terrifying. Then, all at once, she thought of Jesus, the Good Shepherd. He had watched over her and kept her from danger all her life, although only quite recently had she begun to know Him. A feeling of comfort came over her as she realised that He would never forsake her. She did not belong here, but she knew now that she belonged to Him.

CHAPTER THIRTEEN

PLANNING TO RUN AWAY

Gloria, who was usually very talkative, refused to speak to Jo the day after the concert. She found it hard to keep silent, however, and on the following morning the girls were chatting together as usual. Mrs. Pickleworth, too, realised that, in her anger, she had said more than she had ever meant to say, and she made an effort to be kinder to Jo.

Granfer's expected home-call came very peacefully a few weeks later. Mrs. Pickleworth and everyone working at her fair mourned the loss of a kind, wise friend, but the two girls missed him most. Gloria was quite inconsolable for some days. Jo felt the loss of him even more deeply, but she was calmer in her grief. She knew that Granfer was ready to go, and had passed into the fuller life. She realised, too, that death was not frightening as she had once thought it was.

"People like Granfer who belong to Jesus just go to sleep in this world and wake up in heaven," she remarked to Gloria, "and if we belong to Jesus, too, we shall all meet again one day. The Bible says so."

Gloria shrugged her shoulders and did not reply.

The days which followed seemed sad and empty at first, but everyone soon became busy again. The girls went regularly to school, and the fair reopened in the evenings. Mrs. Pickleworth made no further mention of her retirement to Yorkshire. and Jo was relieved to banish from her thoughts the dreaded suggestion that she should run away.

Thanks to regular attendance at school, Gloria's work was improving at last. She was still backward for her age, however, and, although she was two years older than Jo, she had been put into her class.

One afternoon at the beginning of the autumn term, Gloria arrived at school feeling very excited. The day of the music festival had come at last, and that very afternoon Laura was driving her to a small town a short distance away, where it was taking place.

"I'll have to get off quickly when school's over, for Laura can't wait for me long or she'll be late herself," Gloria explained to Jo.

Unfortunately for Gloria, however, when the school bell rang she had not finished colouring a map of South America, and the geography master insisted that she should stay behind and do it.

"Oh Jo, please wait to put away my things afterwards," she implored, as the other boys and girls hurried out of the classroom.

"Okay, unless Miss Bell comes and sends me off," replied Jo.

The colouring was finished with more speed than care, and as Gloria sprang up from her chair to go she knocked over a large plastic jug, and its contents of paint and water flooded the floor near the two girls' desk. At the same moment, Gloria heard Miss Bell approaching, and panic seized her. She would have to get away quickly at all costs, she thought.

"Oh Jo, how clumsy you are!" she exclaimed. "Sorry I can't stop to help you wipe it up," and she dashed out of the classroom, narrowly missing a collision with Miss Bell.

Crimson with indignation, Jo was about to tell Miss Bell that she had not upset the water, and then she suddenly realised that if Gloria were called back she would miss the music festival. This would seem as disastrous to Gloria as missing the art exhibition would have seemed to Jo.

While she stood there, hesitating, Miss Bell entered. "Oh dear! An accident here, then," she said.

"Yes, Miss Bell," Jo replied grimly.

"Well, you know what to get, don't you?"

"Yes, Miss Bell," Jo repeated, as she went out of the classroom. She returned with a bucket and cloth, her face still flushed and angry. It was too bad, she thought. She had been trying so hard to be less clumsy, and she did not want Miss Bell to think that she had been upsetting things again.

It took some time to mop up all the water. Then, when she had almost finished doing so, Miss Bell, who had been arranging books in a shelf, turned round and spoke to her. "Do you remember, Jo," she said, "how last Sunday afternoon we read a text about our Lord, in the fifty-third chapter of Isaiah. It was, 'Surely he hath borne our griefs, and carried our sorrows.' Well, sometimes, in a far lesser degree, we are called upon to suffer for the mistakes of others."

Jo looked up suddenly with a quick smile of gratitude. Miss Bell did understand, then. She knew everything!

When Gloria returned home that night, she went straight to her mother's caravan, much to the disappointment of Jo, who wanted to hear about the music festival. Soon afterwards, Aunt Bella fetched her daughter's bedding.

"Please tell them at the school that Gloria is not very well, and will be away for a few days," she said to Jo.

"I guess it's shock and disappointment that's keeping her from school," a girl in Jo's form remarked next morning.

"But what happened?" asked Jo.

"Well, I was at the music festival," continued the girl, "and Laura came third in that class of fifteen, which was pretty good. Poor Gloria was only one from bottom, though, and she took it badly. The adjudicator said her playing was promising, but she needed proper lessons and lots of practice."

Gloria stayed away from school for nearly a week, and when she went back again she was quieter than usual, and neither the music festival nor the incident of the spilled painting water was mentioned.

One evening, after a long ramble with the three dogs, Jo felt rather tired, and decided to go to bed directly after supper. She had the tent to herself, as Gloria was still sleeping with her mother, and she was glad to feel she would not be disturbed. When Mrs. Pickleworth looked in later, she pretended to be asleep.

Soon afterwards, she heard Aunt Bella talking to a friend just outside the tent. "I am dumping 'er there on Monday," she was saying, "an' I've told 'em she's a big, strong girl, an' they should get plenty of work out of 'er."

Jo shivered with fright when she realised that the conversation was about herself. She strained her ears to hear more.

The other woman said something in a very low voice, to which Aunt Bella replied, "I'll be telling 'er on Monday morning that she's goin' to live with 'er Aunt Hetty."

The two women then moved out of earshot.

Jo's heart was beating very fast. This Aunt Hetty, could she be a real aunt this time? Anyway, Jo did not like the sound of her. Granfer had been right. She would have to run away. Where could she go, though? Her teachers at former schools and Mr. White, the minister, would be kind and sympathetic. Perhaps they would think it their duty, though, to send her back again, as she could not prove that Aunt Bella was not her nearest relation. Also, they might not understand that when one wanted so badly to be an artist one

simply could not spend all one's life cleaning and polishing.

Suddenly, Jo remembered that there was just one
person who would know exactly how she felt, because
he was a real artist. This was Uncle John. It would be
wonderful to see him, and kind Aunt Mary, again,
even if they did have to send her back later. She had
their address, and she had already found out from Miss
Bell the direction in which they lived. She would go
to them.

Sitting bolt upright in bed, Jo began to make her
plans. Miss Bell had said that Oxenmead was about a
hundred miles away, and she knew that Rosewell,
where the Trevellians lived, was twenty miles from
there. Her form mistress had also told her than one
had to go through Newford Gorse to get to Oxenmead,
and she had actually seen a signpost pointing in that
direction.

She hoped to be able to hitch-hike most of the way
there, but she remembered that Granfer had given her
a warning. "Be careful to get into family cars where
there are women and children," he had said to her.

She though next about her belongings. She would
take what she needed in her school satchel. Reluctantly, she decided, though, that she would have to
leave the Bible behind, as it belonged to Gloria. It was
true that the latter would never read it, but perhaps
one day she would, and Jo felt sure Aunt Mary would
help her to get another one for herself.

Jo remembered with relief that she still had not
spent the fifty pence that Aunt Bella had allowed her
to keep from her art prize. This would pay for bus
fares, and for food on the journey, and there was also
the silver rattle to sell when she became short of money.

"I shall want to take some things to eat with me,
too," she said to herself, "for if I go into the shops near
Oakvale, people may recognise me. I'd better stay here

tomorrow, and do things as usual, and every time I have a meal I'll try and save some bread, and put it in my pocket. Then I'll go to bed, just as I always do, and when it is beginning to get light, next day, I'll start off."

Then, worn out at last with so much planning, Jo lay back in bed and fell asleep.

CHAPTER FOURTEEN

ADVENTURES ON THE ROAD

"I'm going away tomorrow," Jo whispered to Cocky, next morning.

"Have a cup of tea, pretty dear," replied the macaw, pecking gently at her hair. "Cocky's a lovely bird," he added.

"I know you are," agreed Jo, "and Gloria thinks so, too, as you'll be okay. Goodbye, Cocky," and Jo hurried off to school.

She was rather absent-minded all that day, but no one appeared to notice this, and she went to bed at last with mingled feelings of terror and excitement. She lay awake most of the night, and at the first glimmer of dawn she dressed quickly in jersey, jeans and sandals, putting on her anorak, too, to save carrying it. Then, picking up the satchel, which was already packed, she crept out of the tent and past the caravans where everyone was sleeping. If Salt, Pepper and Mustard heard her familiar footsteps, they did not bark.

Jo decided to take a short cut to the main road, across two fields and through a wood. When she reached the shelter of the trees, and started walking along the woodland paths, she had an uneasy feeling that she was being followed. It was too dark to see anyone, but now and again she could distinctly hear a soft rustle of leaves and snapping of twigs behind her. Trembling with fear, she made for a thicket of laurel and hid there, hoping the intruder would not see her.

"A clever place to hide in, but you can't trick me!" cried a well-known voice.

"Gloria!" Jo exclaimed in dismay. "I've got to go. You're not going to stop me."

"Oh, keep your hair on," said Gloria, smiling. "I haven't come for that. Do you think I didn't guess you were running away? As for those crusts I saw you slipping into your pockets, well, a mouse would starve on them. That's why I've brought you a meat pie and some sandwiches," she added. "I got them from Laura."

Then, to Jo's astonishment, she handed her a large paper bag.

"But Gloria," Jo stammered, "why are you doing this?"

"Well, if you want to know, it's because you were decent and didn't split on me over that water, and I'm sure now that you didn't let Cocky out on purpose. I know where you are going," she continued. "It's to Mr. White, the minister. He'll put you into an orphanage, I suppose, and you'll probably be happier there, doing things that you like."

"Then you really won't say anything about having seen me?" questioned Jo, anxiously.

"I told you I wouldn't. I can't promise Mum won't try and get you back, though, so you'd better push on before she wakes up and finds you missing."

"And Gloria, could you say goodbye to Miss Bell for me?"

"Okay," replied Gloria. "I'll tell her you don't really belong here, and you've gone away. I told her, yesterday, after school, that I had upset that painting water, and she was decent and talked to me quite a while. She mentioned the youth club that her friend runs, and Laura and I are going to join. There is someone there who gives guitar lessons, too, so it will be super, and I'm telling Mum she's not to move on from here for a long, long time!"

Jo was too surprised and bewildered to reply.

"There's something else," continued Gloria, after

a pause to get her breath. "Miss Bell asked me if I
would go to her Bible class on Sundays."

"And what did you say?" Jo asked, eagerly.

"I couldn't make up my mind at first, but in the end
I said 'yes', and there were two reasons for it," she continued. "One was because Granfer wanted me to go so
badly, and the other was because I noticed that learning about Jesus had made you quite different. You got
happier, and you left off being sulky and spiteful. You
are not quite so horrible as you used to be, now," she
added, with a chuckle.

"Oh Gloria, I'm glad you're going to it," exclaimed
Jo. "I know you'll soon bring lots of other people."

"Well, I'm bringing Laura for a start," said Gloria,
"or maybe she's bringing me, for I would be scared
stiff to go there alone the first time. Now, it's getting
light, and I'd better hop back before I'm seen. Cheerio,
and all the best."

"Cheerio, and thanks a lot," replied Jo.

She watched Gloria's graceful figure disappear
among the trees. Then, with a thankful heart, she ran
through the wood, and out on to the road which she
knew would lead eventually to Newford Gorse.

After walking for two hours, Jo felt very thirsty, and,
passing through a hamlet, she was relieved to find an
old pump and a metal cup attached to a chain close to
it. Eagerly she helped herself to cupful after cupful of
delightfully cool water. She was hungry, too, and real-
ising that she had had no breakfast, she slipped behind
a hedge and, sitting on an old tree-trunk, ate the delicious meat pie that Gloria had brought her, and one of
the sandwiches.

She was about to continue her journey when she
noticed a big boy at the far end of the field, flinging
stones and earth at something small and black which
was moving.

"Horrors! It's a kitten and he'll kill it," she thought,

and the next moment she was rushing in his direction. The boy saw her coming, and picked up the kitten and was about to fling it into a duck pond nearby, when she hurled herself upon him.

The kitten escaped, and the young ruffian fell heavily to the ground. He had, however, grabbed hold of her hair, and was pulling her down, too, when a red-headed boy of about the same age arrived on the scene, and held the ruffian's legs in an iron grip.

"You funk! You miserable rat!" he exclaimed. "You're only brave enough to kill kittens and fight girls."

The bully let go of Jo and screamed in terror as the other boy dragged him to the edge of the pond and then rolled him in. The water was not deep, and the big lad soon struggled out, covered with mud from head to foot.

"I'll tell my dad about you," he wailed.

"Okay. Then I'll tell the R.S.P.C.A. man about you," replied the red-headed boy.

This remark silenced any further threats from the bully, who, with muddy water dripping from his clothes, slouched off, sniffing and sobbing as he went.

The other boy watched him with an amused expression on his round, freckled face.

Jo, in the meantime, had found the kitten under a bush. It was unharmed, and, as she picked it up and fondled it, it started purring.

The red-headed boy joined her.

"Coo! You didn't half give it to him, didn't you?" he chuckled, pointing to the retreating figure of the bully. "I didn't know girls had that much in them."

Jo flushed with pleasure at such praise. "Well, I couldn't have kept the kitten from him much longer, if you hadn't come along," she said. "Anyway," she added, anxiously, "what can we do with him?"

"You don't need to worry," the boy replied. "My

gran goes crazy over cats. She'll have him all right and treat him like a king. Cheerio, then."

Next moment, he was crossing the field with big strides, the little animal tucked comfortably under his arm. Jo glanced ruefully at her anorak. It was now bespattered with mud, and with a tear in the front.

Oh well, she thought, as she found a stream and cleaned herself as well as she could, better this than a drowned kitten.

Very soon she was on the road again. She was afraid to thumb a lift so near Oakvale, and car after car sped past her as she trudged patiently on. By now she was feeling tired and foot-sore, and quite hungry again, so she decided to rest for a while in a shady lane and eat the remaining sandwiches. Then, as she came out again, a car suddenly drew up beside her. It was driven by a young man who had two boys sitting beside him and three girls at the back.

"No need to ask where you are going," he shouted. "Squeeze in quickly, and we'll save you a four mile walk."

Jo obeyed him. She had no idea where she was being driven, but at least it was in the right direction.

One of the boys soon enlightened her. "They've got the big wheel and the fattest man in the world, and candy floss, and hot dogs," he announced breathlessly.

Soon the fairground appeared in sight and the car slowed down. The young man addressed Jo again. "You can go straight in while we are parking," he told her.

"Thank you," was all Jo could reply. She stood for a moment, watching the car turn into a field where many other vehicles were arriving. Then she walked past the fair entrance and was soon out of sight beyond a bend in the road. Both her feet were now hurting, and she was limping badly.

To her relief, another car stopped, and a young girl, who was at the wheel, invited her in.

"What on earth's the matter with you?" she asked. "You were walking like a cat on hot bricks."

"My feet are a bit tired. That's all," answered Jo.

"Well, just yell out when you want me to stop," said the young driver. "I live about half a mile out of Newsford Gorse."

"But that is just where I want to go!" exclaimed Jo, in delight.

"Well, this is your lucky day, then, isn't it?" replied the girl. "There's some smashing pop music on, too," she added, as she turned on a transistor. "You can just sit back and enjoy it, and do finish that bottle of orange squash."

Jo was thankful for the drink, and glad of an excuse not to talk. It was warm and comfortable in the car, and she was soon nodding off to sleep. In what seemed a surprisingly short time, the car stopped with a jerk.

"We are just outside Newford," said the young driver, "and you'd better get out as I'm turning down a lane. It's pouring with rain, you might like to know." she added, "but there are plenty of trees where you can shelter till it's over."

"Goodbye, and thank you very much for the ride," Jo answered, as she jumped out of the car.

Next minute she had climbed over a five bar gate into a field where there were several oak trees. She could hardly believe she was forty miles from Oakvale. No one would recognise her now, she thought. Later on, when the weather was fine again, she would go to the shops and spend part of her precious fifty pence on something to eat and drink. She would also find out if there was a bus that would take her to Oxenmead, or perhaps even to Rosewell.

The rain poured down, and, finding that the trees

were not as waterproof as she had hoped, she cast her
eyes around for better shelter.

Suddenly she noticed a barn at the far corner of the
field, and its door was actually half open. She decided
to make a dash for it, and forgot to be cautious. It was
not until she was nearly inside that she realised it was
already occupied.

CHAPTER FIFTEEN

NIGHT IN A BARN

A cold shiver went down Jo's back when she found she was standing face to face with a very fair-haired girl of about her own height, in faded blue jeans and a scarlet jersey.

"You don't need to look so scared," said the girl, grinning. "I shan't eat you. I'm called Fairy by most people, because of my hair, you see; and I'm fourteen. What's your name?"

"I'm—well, I'm just Jo, and I'm sorry I burst in on you," Jo replied in a shaky voice.

"Not to worry," said Fairy. "This isn't our private property, though it was Peg's and my bedroom last night. She's my pal, and, if you want to know, we've run away together. We were getting fed up with school, and chores at home and everything. It sort of got on top of us. But what are you doing here, by the way?"

Jo was too frightened to reply.

"I know. You don't need to tell me," continued Fairy. "Running away from the cops, aren't you? You'd be surprised if you knew how many times that has happened to me." Then, as Jo still remained tongue-tied, she added, "What do you want to do? Maybe I can help you."

Jo was beginning to feel less uneasy. "I want to eat a hot dog or something, and then get on a bus," she answered.

"That shouldn't be too hard, but hot dogs don't grow on trees round this way. Have you got some cash?"

"Oh yes, thank you," said Jo, feeling for the purse in her anorak pocket. "I shall be all right."

"And where are you going afterwards?"

"I—I—please don't ask me that. I don't want anyone to know," Jo stammered.

"Okay, my darling. Keep your hair on! I wouldn't split on you for worlds. I'll tell you what, though—I'm going to Newford Gorse myself, so I'll show you where you can get some grub, and where the buses start from. Then I'll pop off, like the good little girl I am, and ask no questions."

"Thank you so much, and can we go now?" said Jo, eagerly.

"No, there aren't any buses till later, and I'll have to go and find Peg first. You can have a cat-nap in the hay, and I'll be back for you by five o'clock sharp."

"Are you sure you won't forget?"

"I'll be back all right," replied Fairy, reassuringly, "and I'm leaving my mac in the barn to pick up later, now the rain's over. Don't worry your pretty little head any more. Cheerio, and bye for now."

Jo sank down gratefully on to the soft, dry hay, and in a few moments she fell into a deep sleep. Some hours later, a cow lowing very loudly in a neighbouring field woke her up with a start. Where was she? she wondered. Then she remembered all that had been happening, and sprang to her feet.

She was supposed to be starting off at five o'clock to catch a bus, but she realised that it was now long after that time, as it was beginning to get dark. What could have happened? Why had not Fairy come back to her? Jo looked round the barn and discovered that the mackintosh was gone. Then she must have come back to fetch it, but why had she not kept her promise to Jo? It was all so strange.

Well, anyway, I can't wait for her. I'll have to go on my own, thought Jo. I'll have to buy something to eat, too. I'm famished.

She put her hand in her pocket, and then gave an exclamation of horror. The purse, with her money in it. was not there. She hunted frantically for it, but it had gone. The awful truth dawned on her all at once; the girl was a thief, and had come back and robbed her while she was asleep.

Jo felt very angry suddenly. "The wicked, wicked girl!" she cried. "She never meant to keep her promise. She doesn't care if I starve. I hope she loses all her money, too, and dies of hunger."

Worse was to follow, for Jo soon discovered that the satchel, with all her belongings, including the all-important slip of paper from Mr. Trevellian, was also missing. Foolishly enough, Jo had not memorised Aunt Mary's and Uncle John's address. She knew they lived in Rosewell, but she was relying on that slip of paper for the number of the house and the name of the street. She did not even know how to spell their surname. How could she ever find them now? she wondered. A feeling of utter despair came over her, and she sank down on the hay and burst into tears.

For a short time she lay there, sobbing helplessly. Soon, however, she was up again, and looking out of the barn. What should she do? she wondered. The rain was falling heavily again. It would be too dark and frightening to go to the town alone; and even if she were able to find a bus, she would have no money to pay her fare. The only thing to do was to spend the night in the barn, but she was so terrified of being there alone. How could she bear it? Suddenly some familiar words came into her head: 'In His hands are all the corners of the earth: and the strength of the hills is His also.'

That verse was about God, Jo knew, and He was in charge of everything, but why had she not remembered once that day to ask Him to be with her and help her? She knelt down at once on the hay and prayed. "I am very sorry I have been forgetting about You. Please

make me brave and help me to find Uncle John and
Aunt Mary, although it is going to be terribly difficult."

As she got up from her knees, she felt much calmer.
All the corners of the earth were in God's hand, she
knew, and so He must even be holding her little
corner, with the gloomy barn, and the rain dripping
down from the roof. She thought of Jesus, too—the
Good Shepherd, who took great care of all His sheep,
and she knew she could go to sleep now without being
frightened. Then she began wondering where Fairy
had gone, but all the angry thoughts of hatred and
revenge had now left her. Only pity remained. She
knew that the girl would never have stolen her property if she had belonged to Jesus, and only a short
while ago she herself had stolen all the carrots from a
cottage garden.

Her thoughts flew on to Uncle John and Aunt Mary.
How could she find out exactly where they lived? If
she asked a policeman to help her in her search, he
would guess that she had run away, and would probably take her back again. How could she even get to
Rosewell without food or money?

There did not seem to be any answers to her questions. Nothing was too difficult for God, though. She
remembered how He had even made a way across the
Red Sea for the Children of Israel. He would find a
way for her, too, next morning, and meanwhile she had
a warm, dry place where she could stay till it was light.

Settling down comfortably in the hay, she even
forgot that she was hungry, and was soon fast asleep.

CHAPTER SIXTEEN

A RATTLE TO SELL

The sun was streaming in through the cracks in the old barn next morning when Jo awoke.

For a while she lay comfortably in the hay, stretching her arms and legs and yawning. Then her attention was attracted by a very slight sound near the door, and she saw a tiny brown creature moving about in the hay. At first she thought it was a mouse, and then, suddenly, she noticed that it had a red breast and she knew it must be a robin. It seemed very busy pecking at something.

Jo had noticed on other occasions that robins were often about earlier than other birds, but she wondered what this one could find to eat in the barn. She got up and crept quietly nearer the door to watch it. Then she discovered, to her surprise, that it was pecking greedily at some small pieces of bread which had fallen to the ground. Beside them was a paper bag which seemed oddly familiar.

"My bits of bread!" she exclaimed in surprise. "Just what I need. That girl must have thrown them away because they're rather stale."

She picked up the bag, threw a few crumbs to the robin, which had retreated to a safe distance, and then ate the bread ravenously. While she was doing so, a small, round object at the far side of the barn kept attracting her attention. From that distance it looked like a mushroom growing above the hay, and when she had finished her meal she decided to investigate. Drawing near, she discovered that it was only a bit of crumpled-up paper, but with a cry of surprise and delight she snatched it up. Carefully she smoothed it

out, and there, to her immense relief, still legible, was
Uncle John's and Aunt Mary's complete address. Fairy
had evidently flung this paper out as useless.

"Oh, I've got it, I've got it. I've got it!" Jo exclaimed. "I'll keep it safe always, and I'll learn it by
heart now, too. I'll never be so stupid again."

The retrieving of the all-important address put new
heart into Jo. She tidied herself up as well as she could,
but she wished the girl had left her her comb. Her long
hair was difficult to manage without it.

When she was ready to go, she knelt down and said
the Lord's Prayer, and added to it her thanks for the
recovery of the address. Soon afterwards, she was on
the road again.

As Jo walked along, she discovered to her relief,
that one of her possessions had escaped Fairy's notice.
The old rattle had remained untouched in the pocket
of her jeans. Granfer had told her it was silver, so she
would sell it in the town, and she hoped she would
have enough money then to pay for the food she
needed, and her bus fare.

She soon reached Newford Gorse, and was glad to
see that the little town was awake and busy. At a
butcher's shop a man in a white overall was chopping
up meat, and delicious smells were coming from a
bakery next door.

Jo walked quietly along the pavement, and after
passing a chemist's and a greengrocer's store she came
to what she thought was the very shop where she could
sell her rattle. It had books, games, jigsaw puzzles and
dolls in the window, and there were even small, soft
toys there for babies. She walked straight in and put
the rattle down on the counter.

A middle-aged man with slouching shoulders came
forward and asked what she wanted.

"Would you like to buy this rattle, please?" she enquired.

The man picked up the rattle with his finger and thumb, looked at it hurriedly, and put it down again.

"A rattle, young lady!" he exclaimed. "Do I look as though I want a rattle! What would I do with it, I ask you? Lily!" he shouted to someone behind the scenes. "What a laugh! Did you ever hear the like? A little woman here wants to sell me a rattle—thinks I'm in my second childhood, I dare say. Ha! Ha! Ha!"

Jo did not wait to hear any more. Her cheeks crimson, and with tears of indignation and disappointment springing up in her eyes, she snatched the rattle from the counter and dashed out of the shop. She must get right away, she thought, and not remain a minute longer here, to become the laughing-stock of the town. Anyway, what was the use of staying when she still had no money to spend—and what was the use of the rattle? Granfer couldn't sell it, and she couldn't, either.

Angrily she held it up and was about to fling it down a drain, when she changed her mind. If she managed to clean it up, perhaps she would some day find a baby who would play with it. After all, it was just a baby's rattle.

She had soon left the town behind her, and was walking towards Willow Bridge, the village which she had noticed, on the signpost, was ten miles on the way to Oxenmead.

Jo had not gone very far when she noticed a truck parked in a lay-by. At the back of it there were several pigs, and in the front a fat farmer was sitting with his even plumper wife. Obviously they were on their way to a market, Jo thought, and it would be safe to ask them for a lift.

"I tell you I don't want that pair of goats," the farmer was saying. "You can't have goats and gardens."

"And I tell you I do want them," replied his wife. "I'd see they did no harm."

Jo broke into their conversation. "Please could you give me a lift?" she asked.

"And why not. little missy?" the farmer answered heartily. "There's plenty of room in the front with us, unless you prefer the pigs' company at the back."

Jo smiled. "And could you please give me a drink of water?" she continued.

"Sorry, lassie, we don't carry that about with us." said the farmer's wife, "but we've got something much better—milk from our own Fresians."

She produced a bottle of it from the car, and filled a cup to the brim. Jo drank it gratefully, and when the cup was empty it was filled a second time.

"Oh, thank you! It's super," said Jo.

"And so it should be," agreed the farmer. "Now pack in quickly," he added. "We are off to a farm four miles this side of Willow Bridge. How will that do for dropping you?"

"Fine," answered Jo. "Thanks a lot."

The argument about the advantages and disadvantages of keeping goats then began again, and Jo was glad the couple were too preoccupied to ask her any questions. They dropped her at the bottom of a long, steep hill.

"Go straight ahead for Willow Bridge," they shouted. Then, waving a hurried goodbye to her, they disappeared down a farm lane.

CHAPTER SEVENTEEN

STRENGTH OF THE HILLS

Jo toiled up the steep hill and down another one. Then followed what seemed an endless stretch of level road with common land, where sheep and cows were grazing, on either side.

Her feet were sore again, her legs aching, and a feeling of utter weariness came over her. She struggled on for a while, but found to her dismay that she was getting slower and slower, and would have to rest for a while.

She stepped off the road into a thick clump of bracken, and lay down there where she knew she could not be seen. The morning was warm and windy, and the bracken and ground beneath her felt dry. She tried several times to get up and start off again, only to feel so sick and giddy that she had to go back and rest. Meanwhile, the hours were passing and she was becoming desperately worried.

Supposing I can't go on any more, she thought. Then I shall either starve to death here, or someone will find me and take me to hospital, and then send me back when I am better. Jo did not know which was the lesser of the two evils, and was working herself into a panic.

She threw a terrified glance across the wild common to the gaunt, rugged hills beyond it. Then, again the familiar verse came back to her: 'In His hand are all the corners of the earth: and the strength of the hills is His also.'

"Please, Lord," she prayed, "give me some of Your strength, for I know You are stronger than all the world."

As she left off praying, she heard a clock on a church tower far away in the distance strike two o'clock. The day was going by all too quickly, but she was feeling calmer and better and would try, now, to make up for lost time. She crept out on to the road and started off again at a slow, steady pace.

Jo had only been walking for about five minutes when a car from behind came gliding along very softly and drew up beside her even before she realised it was coming. An old gentleman in a thick, tweed jacket was at the wheel, and beside him sat an old lady with a rosy face and pretty silvery hair. They both greeted her with kind smiles and spoke in low, gentle voices.

"You look very tired, dear," they said. "Would you like a lift with us? We are going to Oxenmead."

Jo could hardly believe her ears. "Oh, how lovely!" she exclaimed, eagerly. "I want to go there, too."

"Jump in then, child," said the elderly gentleman. "There's plenty of room."

Jo climbed in thankfully, and was soon sitting comfortably at the back.

The couple looked such good, friendly people, she thought, but she did hope they wouldn't ask her any awkward questions. for one never knew what grownups might decide to do.

"We have just been staying with our daughter and grandchildren," the elderly gentleman remarked. "We are on our way home now."

The elderly lady then turned round and fixed kind, grey eyes on Jo's pale face. "We are called Mr. and Mrs. Robin," she said. "What's your name, dear?"

"I'm—well—please call me 'Margaret'," Jo replied hurriedly.

"Have you come a long way, Margaret?" Mrs. Robin asked next.

Jo nodded.

"Staying in Oxenmead, I suppose," said Mr. Robin.

STRENGTH OF THE HILLS

"No," answered Jo, looking frightened. "I'm going on a bit further."

Mrs. Robin began to feel very anxious about this girl who was looking so tired and ill. Surely she should not have been out alone on the road in that state, and where would she be spending the night? she wondered. She turned round again.

"Margaret," she said.

Jo was leaning back comfortably, with closed eyes, and the new name did not convey anything to her.

"Margaret," repeated Mrs. Robin.

Jo suddenly recalled, with a start, that she had chosen to be Margaret for the time being.

"Yes, Mrs. Robin," she replied, leaning forward.

"I was wondering, dear, if you were, perhaps looking for work."

Jo shook her head. "Oh, no," she said. "I'm too young. I'm only just twelve."

Both Mr. and Mrs. Robin gave exclamations of surprise.

"My word! You're big for your age!" cried Mr. Robin.

Mrs. Robin was now very worried indeed. If the girl were really telling the truth, and was only twelve years old, she certainly should not be on her own like this; but what could she, Mrs. Robin, do to help without interfering? For a while she was silent, then she turned round once more.

"Margaret, dear," she said. "We don't want to pry into your affairs, but we would like to know where you are planning to spend the night. We have a cosy little spare room, and we would be delighted to have you with us. You look in need of a good meal and a rest," she added, scanning the girl's tired face.

"Thank you very much," Jo answered, hurriedly, "but I'm going to my friends."

"How far beyond Oxenmead do they live?" enquired Mr. Robin.

Jo hesitated. "Quite a little way," she said at last.
"but I shall manage all right."

"How many miles further on?" he insisted.

Mrs. Robin came to the rescue. "Margaret, dear,"
she said. "I am going to tell you where we live in case
you come back to see us. Remember, you will be so
welcome any time, night or day. You need not write
down the address as it is such an easy one to remember.
It is all about birds. We, as you know, are Mr. and Mrs.
Robin, our house is called The Nest, and the little
village near Oxenmead where we live is Birdswalk."

"How funny!" cried Jo, smiling. "I shall always remember that."

Indeed, she thought that the elderly couple with
their rosy complexions and bright eyes were not at all
unlike a pair of robins themselves.

As Jo looked into the old lady's face, which seemed
so full of kindness and real concern on her account,
she felt suddenly that she could confide in her. There
was only one thing, really, that she could not tell her,
and that was that she had run away from home. No one
must know about that except Uncle John and Aunt
Mary, and Jo was even beginning to wonder what *they*
would say when the news was broken to them.

"Mrs. Robin," said Jo, suddenly.

"Yes, Margaret?" replied the old lady.

"My name isn't really Margaret. It's Jo."

"Oh, is it, dear?" said Mrs. Robin, without showing
any surprise. "I expect Jo is short for Josephine, isn't
it?"

"And the place I'm going to," continued Jo, "is
twenty miles the other side of Oxenmead."

Mr. Robin gave a sharp whistle of surprise, and
Mrs. Robin exclaimed in dismay, "Twenty miles! Oh
no!"

"I'll get the address out of my pocket and show it to you," Jo added.

"Yes," agreed Mr. Robin, driving into a lay-by. "I think it is high time we sorted out this matter."

CHAPTER EIGHTEEN

ROSEWELL AT LAST

"Rosewell's the place where my friends live," said Jo, unfolding the scrap of paper and handing it to Mr. Robin.

"Well, you little goose!" he exclaimed. "Why ever didn't you let us know sooner where you were going? We might have driven you miles out of your way."

"But Rosewell is twenty miles the other side of Oxenmead," continued Jo, feeling very puzzled.

"That is where you are mistaken, young lady. It is true it's a distance of twenty miles from Oxenmead, but it happens to be twenty miles this side of it, and, what is more, we shall be arriving there in twenty minutes."

"Oh, Mr. Robin," exclaimed Jo, a flash of excitement lighting her pale face. "Then you'll be taking me all the way?"

"Most certainly we shall," said Mr. Robin, as he started up the car again. "We pass through Rosewell on our way home."

"But this is super. I was getting so tired."

"I am sure you were, you poor child," said kind Mrs. Robin. "You look worn out, dear."

She put on her spectacles and had a look at the address which Mr. Robin had passed on to her.

"Trevellian is the name of your friends, then," she remarked. "We haven't actually met them, but Mr. John Trevellian is quite a famous artist. We have one of his pictures—an exquisite painting of seagulls on wild, rugged cliffs—hanging in our lounge."

Jo smiled with real pleasure.

"I'm glad you've got such good friends," Mrs. Robin continued. "You will hardly want to visit The Robins' Nest now, will you?"

"Oh but I shall, one day," cried Jo, eagerly. "You've been so good to me. I've read a lot in the Bible about God sending angels to help people in trouble," she added, gravely. "I believe He still does, and that you and Mr. Robins are earthly angels, sent to help me."

"Well, I'm afraid I'm not much like an angel," chuckled Mr. Robin.

"Jo dear, I think this is one of the nicest things we have ever had said to us," added his wife. "I only wish it were true. Our Lord set us a wonderful example. He went about doing good, and, young and old, we must all try to follow in His footsteps. If we didn't keep failing and disappointing Him, the world would be a much happier place, wouldn't it?"

They drove on for a while in silence. Then Jo suddenly leant forward and asked, "Mrs. Robin, have you any baby grandchildren?"

"I'm afraid not," answered Mrs. Robin, looking rather surprised, "but why?"

"I've got a rattle in my pocket, to give to a baby," replied Jo.

"Well, that's a very kind thought, and thank you, dear, but my youngest grandchild happens to be eleven years old. I'm afraid he is more interested now in guns and fireworks and dangerous things like that. Sometimes I wish he were small again, and playing with harmless things like rattles."

Jo laughed. "Sometimes I wish I hadn't grown so big, too," she said.

The car, which had been running through pretty wooded country, was now climbing a long, winding hill.

"We are nearly there," remarked Mr. Robin. "Rosewell is very high up, and there are wonderful views all round. Montreux is the house in Chestnut Avenue where you want to go, isn't it?"

"Yes, please," replied Jo.

"Well, I know exactly where the avenue is. Would you like me to drop you at the beginning of it, and let you find the house yourself, or would you rather we came with you in the car?"

"I would like to find it myself, please," said Jo, eagerly.

A few minutes later, after kissing Mrs. Robin good-bye, and thanking the couple for the lift, she was standing on the pavement, waving as the car disappeared round a corner.

Mr. and Mrs. Robin drove away feeling quite easy in their minds now. Jo had the address of her friends who were expecting her, they thought, so everything would be all right.

The fallen leaves rustled under Jo's feet as she walked along the avenue of tall chestnut trees. There were houses on either side, and she kept crossing the road to read the names on the gates. The road was longer than she had expected, and it sloped upwards.

As Jo tried to hurry along, a feeling of weakness and weariness came back to her. Her legs seemed almost too heavy to lift. She must ask someone where Montreux was, she thought. But who? for there did not appear to be anyone about just then. She was anxious, too, about her appearance. What would Aunt Mary think when she saw her uncombed hair and muddy, torn clothes? she wondered.

Climbing higher up the hill, she noticed that some of the curtains of the houses were drawn, so perhaps their occupants were away. Supposing Uncle John and Aunt Mary were away, too, or supposing they were at home but decided that it was their duty to send her back again! Feeling sick with anxiety and dismay, she staggered on until she had almost reached the top of the hill. Then suddenly she noticed a middle-aged woman in an apron, and carrying a mop, coming out of the back entrance of one of the houses.

"Oh, please," Jo exclaimed, "can you tell me where Montreux is?"

"To be sure I can, love," replied the woman, walking out of the gate. "It's the top house on the right. I'm new here, but I've heard tell that a sort of harty crafty gent lives there with his sister, and they're ever so nice. Ah!" she exclaimed, suddenly, "you must be coming to work for them. Their other girl got wed. Now, you won't take it badly if I give you one tip, will you? The lady there is sweet, they say; but she'll be sure to want her helps to be neat and clean."

Jo felt too tired to try to explain the situation. "I— well, I've come a long way," she answered wearily.

"Of course you have, love," the woman answered. "You'll be all right when you're cleaned up, and you're a lucky girl to be getting that job. Now, you see the house I mean, don't you?"

"Yes, thank you. Goodbye," said Jo, anxious to escape any further conversation. She tried to hurry again, but walking became more tedious with every step.

At last she reached a pretty little house, painted green, and standing in its own ground.

A robin was singing its autumn song on a low bush as Jo struggled up the garden path; but she did not see it, for black spots were now appearing before her eyes, and a feeling of giddiness, brought on by hunger and exhaustion, had come over her. The house seemed silent and deserted as she reached the front porch.

"Oh, Lord," she prayed, "I can't go any further. Please, please let them be at home."

She rang the bell and then sank down into a wicker chair which was standing near. There was, what seemed to Jo, a long and terrifying silence. Then, suddenly, she heard the welcome sound of approaching footsteps; the front door was opened, and a gentle voice was exclaiming, "Jo, dear, is it really you? How lovely to see you! But, my poor child, what's the matter? Are you ill?"

"Oh, Aunt Mary, I'm so glad you're here," replied Jo. "I'm all right, really—just tired. That's why I had to sit down."

Aunt Mary glanced anxiously at the girl's white face. "You look quite exhausted, dear," she said, "and when did you last have a proper meal?"

"I can't remember," answered Jo.

"Listen, dear," Aunt Mary continued, "I've got a nice fire burning in the sitting-room, and a sofa for you to lie on. Do you think you could manage to walk there if I helped you."

"Oh yes," agreed Jo, "but I'm too muddy, and I haven't brought anything else to wear."

"Don't worry about that. The dry mud won't do any harm. You're so tall dear, too, that you'll be able to wear some of my clothes later, while yours are being washed. Now," she added, as she put her arm round the girl, "you cling on to me, and we'll see how we get on, shall we?"

Very soon, Jo was lying on the sofa beside a blazing fire. She managed to keep awake to drink the delicious soup which Aunt Mary brought her, but her eyes kept closing.

"I'm longing to hear how you managed to come to us," said Aunt Mary, "but I am not going to bother you with any questions till you've had a good sleep. What about a nice hot bath after that, and a fireside supper together?"

"That would be gorgeous," agreed Jo, "but there is one thing I want to know, please. Where is Uncle John?"

"He is on his way to London in our car," replied

Aunt Mary. "He is spending two nights there with a friend, and they are going to an art exhibition together. Such a pity it had to be just now," she added.

"I see," said Jo, and, next moment, she was fast asleep.

CHAPTER NINETEEN

JO'S STORY

"It's smashing being here," Jo remarked, some hours later.

The thick, blue dressing-gown which Aunt Mary had lent her matched the colour of her eyes, and the fleecy-lined bedroom slippers which she wore were just her size. She was certainly feeling much better. Her cheeks were rosy again, and her long hair, now well brushed and combed, shone in the firelight.

"Are you sure you are all right now?" Aunt Mary enquired, anxiously.

"Oh yes, thank you," Jo replied, "and so I ought to be, after all you have done for me."

"It's such a pleasure to have you with me, dear," Aunt Mary continued, "but I can't think how you managed to get here. Did you walk and hitch-hike all the way?"

Jo nodded.

"But it was most risky and unsuitable. It was kind of your aunt to spare you, but I think it was foolish and wrong of her to let you come like that."

"But she didn't let me come," said Jo, bluntly. "I ran away."

"You ran away, dear!" exclaimed Aunt Mary, looking suddenly shocked and worried. "Your aunt doesn't know you are here, then? Oh Jo, we must get in touch with her. She will be anxious about you."

"She won't!" said Jo. "Anyway, she is not my real aunt; she told me so."

"That makes no difference, dear. She is in charge of you."

"But she isn't any more, for she's sending me away

to someone called Aunt Hetty, and I'm sure she's not a proper aunt, either."

"Well, anyway, they have more claim on you than I have, unfortunately. Dear Jo, I do hope you understand how much I would like you to live here altogether. I hate the thought of parting with you again. I can't help feeling it's my duty, though, to get a telephone message delivered to your people, to let them know you are safe and well."

"But you can't, really you can't!" exclaimed Jo, turning pale again. "They are living out in the fields and there's no telephone anywhere near. Please, please leave them alone."

"Oh dear!" exclaimed Aunt Mary, "I wish I knew what to do for the best. If only my brother were here. He will be arriving in London soon, though, and then I'll telephone him. I am sure he will know what should be done."

"Auntie," cried Jo, anxiously, "you couldn't possibly send me back in a car or anything tonight, could you?"

"No, dear," said Aunt Mary, putting her arm round her. "You wouldn't be well enough."

"And you'll let me stay with you tomorrow, too, won't you, for my clothes could never be washed and dried in time to go."

"Yes, darling, if I have to send you back, I am sure it will not be tomorrow. Now we won't worry about this any more for the present."

"But Auntie," Jo implored, "please, please promise me one thing."

"What is it, dear?"

"You won't let me go away, will you, till Uncle John come back. I want to see him so badly."

"Very well, Jo, you shall stay here, anyway, till he returns, and now I am longing to hear about all your adventures. Do, please, tell me everything."

With the exception of Granfer, Jo had never known anyone so sympathetic and easy to confide in as Aunt Mary. There were no secrets to keep back from her, and soon Jo was not only giving an account of her long and difficult journey, but was mentioning, also, her life with Aunt Bella, and her reason for running away.

"You couldn't really blame Aunt Bella for wanting to pass me on to that other aunt," she remarked. "I was pretty awful before I learnt about Jesus, what with shoplifting and being jealous of Gloria, and trying to hurt her. Then when I became a Christian, I still wasn't much use there, for I couldn't do the things I was supposed to do.

"Oh, Auntie," she exclaimed, suddenly, "if I do have to go to Aunt Hetty. I know I shall have to try to help her, but I don't think I could bear to scrub floors and clean out caravans all my life. I do so want to become an artist."

"You poor girl," said Aunt Mary, with tears in her eyes, "you have so many problems and difficulties, haven't you? I am quite sure, though, that God knows about them, and will sort them all out for you in His good time."

"Anyway, I know now that He is always with me," Jo replied, "and I don't get frightened any more."

"It was certainly wonderful how you were cared for and brought safely here," continued Aunt Mary.

"Yes," agreed Jo, "and I hadn't any money to pay for anything, either. The only thing I had left was a rattle."

"A rattle?" repeated Aunt Mary, in surprise.

"Yes, and when I tried to sell it the shop man laughed at me, and I was so angry I nearly threw it down a drain. It is still in my anorak pocket. Would you like to see it?"

"Yes, please," said Aunt Mary, smiling.

Jo darted out to the cloakroom to fetch the rattle,

and next minute she had dropped it into Aunt Mary's lap. "You can keep it," she said, "and perhaps you'll find a baby, some time, who'll like it. Granfer said it's silver. as there's a lion on it. It has a tiny picture of a cat, too—at least, it is supposed to be one, for it has C.A.T. written under it. It doesn't look much like a cat, though, does it, and I'm sure I could draw a better one."

As Jo chattered on, she did not notice that Aunt Mary's hands were shaking as they held the rattle, and that her face had become quite white.

"Jo," she suddenly exclaimed, almost fiercely, "tell me at once, please—how did you get this rattle?"

Jo started and looked at her in surprise. "I didn't steal it, if that's what you mean," she cried.

"Of course not, child, but tell me quickly, please, how it came into your possession."

"But it has always been mine," said Jo, "except that Granfer kept it for a bit. Oh, I forgot to tell you, didn't I, what happened to me when I was very small? My mother died, you see. She was drowned, and Granfer found me on the edge of a cliff, and the rattle was with me, too, when he saved me."

Aunt Mary was now trembling all over. "I—I must telephone my brother," she stammered. "Can you do a sketch while I am busy, dear? There's paper and a pencil on the writing table."

"Yes, but what shall I draw?" asked Jo.

"Cows in a field," replied Miss Trevellian, hardly knowing what she was saying. Then, rather unsteadily, she walked out of the room.

CHAPTER TWENTY

THE LION AND THE OTTER

"I wonder what's the matter with Aunt Mary? I hope she's not getting ill," Jo said to herself, as she started sketching.

In the foreground she drew a large field with oak trees on either side of it. At the back there was a farm-house, and above it a sky with big, fluffy clouds sailing across it.

Auntie's a long time, thought Jo. Oh dear! I've forgotten about the cows. I'll put some under the trees.

Jo drew four cows and then held the picture up to the light. "The cows look very queer," she told herself. "What's the matter with them? Oh, how silly I am! I've given them all horses' legs."

"Is Auntie ever coming back?" she questioned, as she rubbed out all the legs and had another try. "I wonder if I'd better see how she is getting on."

This time the cows looked even more peculiar. "Wow!" exclaimed Jo. "They've all got lions' legs now. I can't draw for toffee tonight. I wish Uncle John was here. He'd soon put things right for me."

At that moment, Aunt Mary came in again. She was quite composed now, and Jo thought she looked very well.

"Jo, darling," she said, sitting down beside her. "I have some very good news, but I must break it to you gently. I have been made wonderfully happy, but so suddenly that it came as a shock, and I must not let that happen to you."

Jo looked puzzled. "I don't know what you mean," she said.

"Well, dear, I—well, I want first to talk to you about this rattle."

"But I know all about it, and it's awfully dull, Auntie," sighed Jo. "It has a lion and a very poor cat on it, and that's all."

"The animal you think is a cat is really an otter, though," replied Aunt Mary, "and it is my grandfather's old family crest. The otter appeared on all his silver, china and notepaper, and on many other articles, and when he died some of his silver, including this rattle, was passed on to me."

"Then why does it say it's a cat if it's an otter?" asked Jo.

"But it doesn't, darling. The C.A.T. are initials. and they stand for Catherine Ann Trevellian."

"That's not your name, though, Auntie," said Jo, feeling more and more puzzled.

"No, dear, it is not. I had those letters engraved on the rattle myself to give to my baby niece. Baby Catherine's mother," Aunt Mary continued, almost in a whisper, "died a long time ago."

"Like my mother did," added Jo.

"Yes, and although we knew she would be living in perfect peace and happiness, the sorrow of losing her seemed almost more than my brother and I could bear. We were living in a little seaside village on the west coast of Wales, then, but he and I had gone together to an art ehxibition in Paris when the accident happened. Baby Catherine's dear mother fell over a cliff on a foggy afternoon, and was drowned."

"But that's what happened to my mother," exclaimed Jo, as she slipped a hand into one of her aunt's, and clasped it tightly.

As Aunt Mary looked up, she noticed a flash of excitement on the girl's face.

"Oh, Auntie," whispered Jo, "I think I can guess the rest of the story now, but please go on. I want to hear you tell it, and know it is really true."

"Very well," said Aunt Mary, in a shaky voice. "We

grieved so much, too, for baby Catherine, who was
with her mother at the time of the accident, for when
the pram was washed up on the shore everyone was
certain that she had been drowned, too. God, in His
mercy, looked after her, though, on the very edge of the
cliff, and her silver rattle told the true story long
afterwards."

"And her rattle is my old rattle, isn't it, and I am
really Catherine? Isn't it simply wonderful?" Jo exclaimed, as she flung her arms round her aunt's neck.

"Yes, darling. You are Catherine Ann Trevellian,
but you'd better still be Jo tonight, so that we can get
used to the new names by degrees."

"Then you are my real aunt now, aren't you?"

"I most certainly am."

"I shan't ever have to go away, then, shall I?"

"Of course not, my dear. This is your home. You
belong here."

"How gorgeous! With you and Uncle, and in a
house that isn't on wheels," Jo sighed contentedly.

Then, for a while, she remained silent, quite over-
whelmed by all the happiness which had so suddenly
flooded into her life.

"Oh, Auntie," she cried at last, "God has answered
the prayers which I used to think He never would
answer. He has made a path across the Red Sea for
me, just as you said He would."

"Yes, dear, and He has reminded me, too, that just
as He watched over a helpless baby on a bleak cliff-top
so He will be beside each one of us, if we ask Him,
every step of our lives."

"There is one thing I am still longing for," Jo
continued, after a pause, "and that is to see Uncle
John again. He's my real uncle now, too, isn't he?"

"No, Jo, you are wrong there. He is not your uncle,"
replied her aunt.

A sudden feeling of disappointment and dismay

came over Jo. "But he must be my uncle," she answered, almost defiantly, "for he's your brother, isn't he?"

Aunt Mary smiled. "He isn't your uncle, though," she insisted. Then, noticing the girl's troubled face, she added quickly, "He's a much nearer relation to you than that, my darling. He's your own father."

"My dad, my very own dad!" Jo exclaimed in wonder.

"What is more, I have telephoned him and told him the news, and he simply can't wait to see his young daughter. He is on his way back now, and should be here in less than two hours."

"Oh, how simply super!" cried Jo.

Springing to her feet, she danced round the room, upsetting a flower vase.

"I'm sorry, Auntie," she exclaimed. "Shall I get a cloth and wipe up the water?"

"No, dear, let it drip on to the carpet. It doesn't matter. Nothing like that matters tonight," was the rather unexpected reply.

"I haven't really got an Aunt Hetty, have I?" asked Jo, looking serious for a moment.

"Certainly not. I am your only aunt. We have no Hetty and no Bella, either, in our family."

"And Dad was never a trapeze artist, was he?"

Aunt Mary burst out laughing. "No, darling," she cried. "The very idea of your dad walking a tight rope! He wouldn't be able to do it if he tried for a thousand years. You are rather like your mother was when she was a girl," she added. "We played together long ago, and when I met you at your art competition I had a feeling I had seen you before. Now I know why."

"And what was Daddy like when he was my age? Am I a bit like him, too?"

"Yes. He was enormously tall, just as you are, dear,

and his long arms and legs always seemed to be getting in the way."

"Was he just a little bit clumsy, sometimes, then?" asked Jo, eagerly.

"I should say he was very clumsy indeed. In fact, he was always knocking things over."

"Just like me, then!" exclaimed Jo, her eyes shining. "Oh, Auntie, I'm so glad!"